Shh...

BEWARE OF THE SNITCH KILLER

BY DADDY RICH

Dedication

This book is dedicated to Zar Dyson. Hold ya' head up and keep fightin' nigga. You a gangsta and don't ever forget it. Love ya cuz.

(For those of you who don't know, the police tried to kill him. They shot him multiple times, several shots in the back and instead of airliftin' him to the nearest trauma hospital according to procedure, they drove him in hopes that he died. But guess what coppers, he made it and justice will run it's course.)

Acknowledgments

All praise is due to Allah! A big thanks goes out to my wife Taneisa. Thanks for your continuing love and support. I know you've made many sacrifices to ride this prison sentence out wit' me. It's been 6 long years. Insha Allah (GOD willing) I'll be home soon.

To Blackstone and Tre, I miss ya'll niggaz. Ya'll were the first people to come back *Geeked!* Talkin' 'bout how good my shit is, tellin' me I'm a real author. I'll never forget the support ya'll showed me. I'm around a bunch of snakes and haters right now, and it makes the support ya'll gave me more real. I love ya'll niggaz, real talk.

I want to send a big thanks to Ruben Peirson (Throwback) and Louis Rayford for puttin' the soundtrack together. Thanks to my nigga Freddie Gibbs for slidin' me a couple tracks and congrats on your deal wit' CTE. Much love.

Cheryl, thank you so much for everything you've done for Gangsta-Lit and www.urbanimagemagazine.com. You have been more than a writer for my magazine. My wife and I view you as family. Thanks. I also want to thank the rest of my staff at Urban Image: Jeff, Emiaj, and Christopher Brown. Thanks for all you do to make the magazine a success. Last but not least, I wanna thank my family. My mom, my dad, my baby sis (Nikki) and my grandma. I love ya'll and I miss ya'll so much. To my kids; I don't care what nobody tells ya'll. Daddy loves each and every one of you. That's why I fought so hard at trial, and that's why I sit down and write 12 hours a day, so I can support you guys. You'll see, I got big plans. Kia, Oshiana, D'zhae, Stacia, Lil' Richarh, Que'Sean, Que'Aundre and Ashya, I love you and I'm tryin' to come home.

Oh shoot, I almost forgot. Thanks to my Aunt Nae and Helen for the support ya'll showed me when I dropped Mack's Revenge. I love ya'll. Helen, I know you gonna like this one too. It's the shit, I promise. And most importantly, I wanna thank YOU—the ones reading this. The ones who bought my book. Thanks. Hit me up on twitter @Gangstalit and on Facebook and visit my website at www.gangsta-lit.com. Fuck wit' ya boy I'm really trying to connect wit my fans. I will hit you back! I'm sorry if I forgot anybody.

~Daddy Rich has done it again! He has penned another street novel that's sure to be a hood classic. He drags you into the plot. You are sure to be driven by suspense and curiosity as this page turner grabs your attention from beginning to end.

-Tyson: Black and Nobel

~Electrifying! "Shh" is an erotic thriller with mind blowing sex scenes. Daddy Rich narrates in a Midwestern drawl that pulls you into the streets of Indiana. I couldn't put it down!

-Terry L Wroten: CEO of No Brakes Publishing and bestselling author of "NATURAL BORN KILLAZ", "TO LIVE & DIE IN LA" & the highly anticipated novel "GIRL, I HAD ENOUGH"

"Prologue"

Gary Tribune, Monday September 20th 2010.....

Convicted drug dealer and confirmed gang member Ryan "R-Dubb" Williams, 33 of Gary, will be released from the Indiana State Penitentiary in Michigan City this morning. Three months ago, the Indiana Court of Appeals overturned his 2004 conviction for selling an eighth of a kilo to confidential informant #976 Norman De'Wayne Sanders, also known as "Big D". The court cited ineffective assistance of counsel stating Williams' constitutional rights were violated due to the sub-standard performance of his defense counsel. They ordered the Lake County Circuit Court to conduct a new trial.

However, before a trial could be held, the confidential informant's 13 year old niece found him murdered inside his sister's home. His throat had been cut from ear to ear. The killer "dropped a dime" on his chest and the phrase "Speak No Evil" was written on the wall in his own blood. Because of the informant's inability to testify at trial, all charges against Williams were dropped. Neither the Prosecutor's Office, nor Judge Wakenhut could be reached for comment.

CHAPTER 1

A few days later...

"Do you love me?" Nicole asked as she laid on Ryan's chest after a hot and steamy sex session.

"You know I do baby," Ryan responded, kissing her on her forehead, rubbing his fingers through her hair.

"I waited on you for five long years, layin' alone at night playin' wit' my pussy, sleeping wit' a pillow in between my legs, feinin' for you to come home. I'll never let anyone take you from me again, you hear me?" she responded, looking deep into his eyes.

"You ain't gotta worry about *nothin'* Mommi, I promise."

"I know it. I'm gonna do my part. Whatever it takes to see you on top, that's what we gonna do. Look at me," she said, gently touching his chin, guiding his eyes to meet hers. "Don't forget, *I'm* that bitch. *I* held you down while all them *ho's* you thought were your girlfriends was runnin' round here gettin' pregnant. I worked doubles, saved my money and gave you my tax checks to pay them lawyers to get you home. *I* snuck you packages to the guards and up in that visiting room to make sure you had plenty to eat and whatever else you wanted. *I* bought cell phones and paid $700 a month phone bills for *five* years nigga . . . "

"So you throwin' it all in my face now?" Dubb butted in.

"Shhh, just listen to what I'm trying to tell you baby," she said, placing her nicely manicured fingers to his lips to quiet him. "I'm not throwing it in your face. I did it all because I love you and I wanted to. I wanted you to come home with me. I just want you to remember who held you down when all these skanks start throwin' pussy in your face. You got all the pussy you need right here," Nicole said as she took his hand and placed it between her legs. "I need you to go down there and show Mommi how much you appreciate her," she said, guiding her man's head down between her thighs. Hungry for her sweet, sticky juices, Ryan didn't hesitate to part her pussy lips wit his index and middle fingers, licking her moist slit up and down wit' long strokes of his tongue. Nikki opened her legs wide, sittin' up on the bed and holdin' Dubb's face in her hands. She grinded her kat in a slow sensual rhythm as he gripped her by her ass and ate her out. He licked and sucked, takin' the time to massage her swollen clit in between his lips.

"Eeew shit! Eat that pussy baby," Nikki coached him as she sat up on her elbows watchin' Dubb eat her out. She threw her legs out to the side and laid back making love to his face, moaning and crying out in pleasure as her sweet smelling nectar oozed out of her pink sugar hole drippin' on Ryan's chin while he continued to give her his mouth.

"Oh shit Dubb, oh baby, I'm gonna cum, oh I'm gonna cum, open your mouth baby, oh shit, oh shit, Mommi gonna cum in your mouth! Oh shit, shit, I'm cummminnnn!! Ooooooh shit!," she screamed, clawing the back of his head as she came in hard, intense spasms. She pulled his face from in between her pussy lips to her mouth, kissing him wit' sheer passion, enjoyin' the taste of her own sweet pussy on his lips. Then she looked deep into his eyes.......

"On my Mamma, if you *ever*, in yo' muh fuckin' life, give my mouth, my dick, or any of your time to *any* of these stank ass bitches, I will kill you! I paid for you nigga. I bought you for

$90,000. That's lawyer fees, commissary, phone bills, shoes, gas, and maintenance on my car drivin' up and down the highway every other week to see you. You mines nigga, *and* I got papers on yo' ass since we married now. That's *my* name on yo' neck."

"And that's my name on yours," Ryan responded, lovin' Nikki's aggressiveness. It has always turned him on.

"You damn right that's your name on my neck, and I wear it wit' pride too. You ain't never got to worry about me baby. I'm different from these other bitches. Hell yeah I'm claimin' you, but I ain't got no problem holdin' you down, satisfying all yo' needs. A *real* bitch can claim her nigga when she's handlin' her muh fuckin' biz'ness. So play if you want. You cheat on me—I'll kill you," she said, squeezing R-Dubb's dick lookin' him dead in the eyes.

This bitch crazy. Dubb thought to himself.

CHAPTER 2

Task foce headquarters.......

"How's it goin' Charles?" the sergeant asked as he approached the evidence cage.

"It's goin' good. What can I do for you sarge?" Charles asked.

"I need evidence, tag number 1139A09," the sarge responded.

"Hang on a second," Charles said as he went to retrieve the latest evidence resulting from a drug bust--12 kilos of cocaine seized from a dope dealer transporting cocaine from East Chicago to Gary.......

"Here you go," Charles said sliding the sergeant the evidence bag without having him sign for it.

"Thanks," he said winkin' at Charles as he took the evidence bag from the window, inconspicuously givin' Charles 10 crisp hundred dollar bills in a handshake. "Congratulations on your retirement. I heard you get to call it quits early."

"Yeah, I'm outta here. I'm movin' out to Colorado. Im'a live up in the mountains," Charles responded.

"Good luck," the sarge said as he turned and walked away.

"4 or 5 hours sarge....tops!" Charles yelled after him as he left.

"Yep," the sarge responded, waving his hand. He kept walkin' towards the rear exit in the basement of the task force's headquarters located on the south side of Chicago. It's located between a chop shop and a carry-out fish restaurant.

Sarge is a member of a highly undercover joint task force. His jurisdiction covers Chicago, East Chicago, Gary, and Hammond. The *regular* police don't even know who the members are, but fuck tha police! Sarge is a cop--Detective Sergeant to be exact--but he couldn't give a *fuck* about the police or bein' a cop. He was groomed from his childhood on up to *infiltrate* the police force so he could feed information and dope to his family. His loyalty is to the streets, his uncle, and his brother.

Sarge reached in his pockets for his keys and hit the locks on his black on black 2008 BMW i750 sittin' on 22 inch black and chrome Lexani rims. This is his undercover vehicle until he decides he wants something else.

Sarge hopped in and got on the highway headed to his lil' traphouse in G.I. to cut the dope he just took from the evidence room. He hit play on the disc player and started bangin' "Money to Blow" by Birdman featuring Drake and Lil' Wayne. He fired up a Swisha filled wit 'dro as he relaxed in the cockpit of his ride, grippin' the steerin' wheel, admiring the woodgrain.

To the police? Sarge is a hardnosed cop wit' a street edge that helps him sniff out dope dealers. In his heart though he's a gangsta, a street nigga, a kick do' artist who singles out Mark ass niggaz (informants who still think it's cool to be a snitch *and* sell drugs) and dope dealers who don't wanna pay their "taxes".

BEWARE OF THE SNITCH KILLER

He's just ridin' along the highway, gangsta shit vibratin' through the 12 inch subwoofers in the trunk of the beemer as he tapped on the wheel, astounded by the sun glistenin' off the 5 carats in his pinky ring. After 40-45 minutes and two Swisha's, he approached the exit for G.I., takin' it and cruisin' through the deadly streets stoppin' in the driveway of his "trap house".

He got out the ride and entered the house located in a nice, quiet, middle class neighborhood. The crib was seized from a mid-level dope dealer a few years ago. Sarge copped it at a police auction. He don't never stay there. He just uses it for a spot to cut dope and stash shit.

The sarge went strait to work bustin' 2 of the bricks down in large storage tubs, mixin' em' wit' creatine and bakin' soda. He vacuum packed a kilo at a time wit' one of those vacuum air compressor, sealer thangs you use to suck all the air out of meat so it won't get freezer burnt. Sarge worked like a pro as he looked at his watch, knowin' his brother'll be at the do' in 35-40 minutes. He took 12 ki's from evidence and took two of em' and turned em' into 12 bricks of strait boo-boo. Garbage! A muh fucka'll shoot up ya, *grandmamma's* house for sellin' em' that shit! It's just enough cocaine in there for it to test positive when it gets sent to the lab, and true enough, just as sarge got through packagin' up the cocaine and cleanin' up his mess, his brother was at the do'.

"What's up bruh? I see you lookin good. You put on some *weight* nigga. What the fuck was they feedin' you up in there?" Bryan asked sizing up his paternal twin as he let him inside.

"Aw shit, I was in there hittin' that iron. Stayin' in shape.

That and reading. Ain't shit else to do."

"How Uncle Nook up in there doin'?" (Uncle Nook an old school El-Rukn. He doin' a life bid for killin' a cop from Chicago back in the 70's. Word is, that he was hooked up wit' some dirty cops out of Gary. They had some shit poppin' off. They was stealin' dope out the evidence room and givin' it to Uncle Nook and 'nem to sell. A lot of shit was comin' up missin' out the evidence rooms in G.I., East Chicago, and the Chi. The cop from Chi-Town was some good Samaritan ass nigga who was getting a lil' too "nosey". He brung his ass down from Chicago while he was off duty tryin' to investigate on his own. Tryin' to play some super-cop shit. Uncle Nook got the phone call and he went and handled that shit. Big Nookie held solid. He didn't "rat" on the cops. They were all homeboys who grew up in the same projects who ended up with different "careers". They did what they could do for Big Nookie. They saved him from the electric chair, but they couldn't keep him out the penitentiary.)

"Shiiit, he doin' good. He's peaceful," R-Dubb responded.

"That's good, that's good. So how's Ms. Nikki Thompson doin'? I know she's happy you got out," Bryan asked.

"It's Mrs. Williams now. That's your sister-in-law bruh. We went to the courthouse and got married the same day I got out."

"For real? Congratulations bruh! Why didn't ya'll wait and have a real weddin'?" Bryan asked, wishin' he could've been there.

"Shit, for who? I wasn't payin' all that money for no ceremony for all my fake ass family and friends. Everybody cut out bruh. After that judge gave me 40 years, everybody left. All the ho's, all the homies, everybody man. Momma gone. We couldn't have nobody findin' out we was brothers, so we couldn't keep in touch like we wanted. The only person I had on the outs was Nichole," R-Dubb explained to his brother while trying to conceal the deep hurt inside his heart from being abandoned. "So we just did our thang."

"She's a good girl Dubb. I'm happy for you. Welcome home baby boy, welcome home."

"Thanks B," R-Dubb said as him and his brother exchanged hugs.

"Everything's in order," Detective Sergeant Bryan Wilkins of the Metropolitan Joint Task Force said as he handed his twin brother the suitcase. "There's 10 kilo's in there. Do what you do. Just give me a hundred grand. Take your time and be careful. I got your back. You don't have to worry about the task force. I can tell you all the task force's moves, when they comin', and if you're bein' watched. I can even tell you who the informants are, but you still have to be careful and watch out for that nigga James. Everything's gonna work out now I'm on the task force."

"You mean J.G.?" Dubb asked.

"Yep, James Griffin. The Captain got it approved last week. It's all clear with the D.A.'s office. He got released this morning. They're pissed. They think you ordered a hit on that C.I. on your case. Their main objective is to send you right back to prison. They think you had it all planned out to win a new trial then have the C.I. murdered."

"Shit, I just got lucky bruh. I didn't have nothing to do wit that shit," Ryan said as him and his brother locked eyes, quietly agreein' not to discuss it any further.

"However it went down, they're dropping J.G.'s charges in exchange for him agreeing to set you up. So watch that nigga. He told us everything he knew about you from the time ya'll niggaz was stealin' candy from Handy Dandy's all the way up to you traffickin' cell phones in the joint," Bryan said.

"It's cool. I'll spin the nigga. I'll tell him I ain't doin' nothing," Ryan said.

"Be careful bruh, I don't want our shit getting busted up like Uncle Nook's and nem' shit back in the days when we was little. I can't believe it, we *doin'* this shit! I still remember when Uncle Nook sat us down and told us he needed me to be a cop, make it to Detective. I was jealous when he told us you was the one cut out for the streets. Now look at you. You a well known and respected Vice Lord out there getting money. I love you bruh. Be careful," Bryan said.

"I love you too bruh. It's good to be home, damn good to be home," Ryan said as he turned and walked out the do'. He got to the passenger side of Nikki's Aurora and got in. He threw the bag in the back, kissed his wife on the cheek, and she drove off.

"How's 'B' doin?" Nikki asked.

"He doin' good. He said congratulations and he's happy for us. He's mad he couldn't be there though."

"Aww, I wish he could've been there too. I love ya' brother. He came through wit' a few ends here and there. He even helped wit' the lawyer a lil' bit, but the rest of your people ain't shit. I couldn't get help from nobody," she said as Dubb kept his true feelings to himself. He knows his brother had the money to pay his lawyer 10 times without even flinchin'. He could've been out.

"It's all good baby, I'm home now," he said pattin' her knee.

"How much he give you?" Nikki asked as she continued to drive.

"We got 10 ki's. I gotta slide bruh 100 G's when I get done."

"Hell yeah. We finna come up baby," Nikki said, eyein' the road. "I need one and I'll have the money in a day or two. 'Til death do us part nigga," Nichole said, lookin' over at her husband, flashin' her beautiful smile.

"Til death do us part," he responded, smiling right back at her lil' sexy ass. Dubb and his wife swore on everything they love that they comin' up *together,* just the two of em'. Dubb ain't finna go fuckin' wit' none of his so-called homies or none of that shit. Wasn't none of these niggaz around when he was down needin' lawyer money. Why put 'em on? *Fuck that! I'm plugin' wit real ass niggaz I was locked up wit* Dubb thought to himself.

"This the *shit*! We got a license to hustle baby. Long as we don't get stupid wit' our shit we cool. Wit' ya' brother tippin' us off, we can't go wrong," Nichole said. She was all excited-n-shit thinking of the come up her and her hubby 'bout to make. Realizin' her loyalty is about to pay off, she's makin' a long list of shit she wants, and it's well deserved. She's spent the last 5 years doin' wit'out all the extras and nice shit like getting her hair and nails did, goin shoppin', and buyin' nice clothes. She pinched every penny she had to keep money on Dubb's books, the phone, and pay sheisty ass lawyer after sheisty ass lawyer.

"Shit, now that you said something, don't tell that bitch Ja'Mesha nothing. None of our bid'ness or nothing. Don't fuck wit' her. Don't sell her shit. I hear she been tryin' to hustle lately."

"I don't even fuck wit' her like that, but why? What's wrong?" Nichole asked as they got caught by a light.

"Bryan told me they cut her brother James loose in order to set me up. They dropping all his charges. That nigga is out," Dubb responded with frustration.

"Hmmmph, faggot ass nigga. I swear these niggaz is weak. Ain't that your homeboy from like, ele'mentry school-n-shit?"

"Yep" Dubb answered.

"Boy I swear, these niggaz out here got pussy in between they legs," Nichole said as she made a left turn.

"Niggas get caught up and tell something first chance they get. The nigga come 'round me askin' 'bout some dope I'm a burn em' ," Dubb responded.

"That nigga was in too much bullshit, robbin' and shootin' people befo' he got locked up. To many niggaz wanna merk his ass. Soon as they find out he on the bricks, *somebody* gonna get his ass watch."

"These niggaz ain't gonna do shit," R-Dubb said as they

pulled up to the crib.

"Bet some head. If that nigga make it on the streets a week, I'll suck yo' dick 'til my jaw hurts. If he don't, I want you to lick ice cream off my pussy, bet?" Nichole asked stickin' out her hand.

"Bet," Ryan said shakin' her hand. Now let's go up in here and bust some of this work down……

CHAPTER 3

Later that night........

"Hell yeah, hell yeah baby, suck that dick, suck it," James "J.G." Griffin said as his baby mama Simone gave him some head while he laid back on the bed at the Merrillville Inn. He's in heaven right now.

Just less than a week ago, he thought he'd never see daylight. When the detectives came to the Lake County Jail to see him, he just couldn't refuse their offer. Walk free? All his bitch ass has to do is make a few nice sized purchases of cocaine from his homie Ryan "R-Dubb" Williams and he's a free man. *Better him than me. I'm 'bout tired of Dubb's ass anyway. Hoggin' all the shine, all the bitches. Always gotta be number 1. Fuck it.* He thought to himself tryin' to justify the bullshit he finna do while he's getting his dick sucked........

"Oh shit, gotdamn girl! 'Lemme get up in that pussy," J.G. said as he got up, layin' Simone down on her back, pullin' her to the edge of the bed so he could stand up and hit that pussy. He cocked her legs up on his shoulders and stuck his dick in her juicy slit. He thought he'd *never* fuck his baby mama again. *Aw shit, it feels good,* he thought as he began humpin' her in short quick strokes.

"Oh shit James, get this pussy baby, oooh, I need you to get this pussy," Simone said layin' on the bed spreadin' her legs wide open while rubbin' her clit in lil' circles. Simone is a sexy, light-brown skinned bitch, wit' natural blondish brown hair she wears in a long kinky afro-type style. She keeps a neat lil' blondish brown bush on her pussy. She reminds you of "Unique", ole girl from the 1st season of For the Love of Ray J except she got fuller lips.

"Hell yeah baby, aw *hell* yeah! Aw shit Simone, I'm gonna........AAAAAAgh shit! Damn baby, I came!" James said in embarrassment as his lil' dick went limp inside Simone's hot, throbbin' pussy.

"You punk!" Simone yelled at him as she punched him in the arm. "Is that it nigga? Hell, I was better off playin' wit my pussy while I was suckin' ya' dick," she said. She was mad as hell and got up to put her clothes on. "Nigga you ain't shit! I'm hungry, give me some money so I can go get me some chicken," she said, goin' in his pants pockets. *Wish his lil' punk ass never got out,* she thought to herself. *He don't hit this pussy like John John do.*

"Cool, get me a pack of blunts and a pint of Hennessy," he ordered from the bed like he done really put it down.

"I shouldn't get yo' weak ass shit. Maybe the Henny'll make you fuck better," she said. She snatched her keys and her purse and headed out the do', slammin' it behind her.

I guess I'll hop in the shower and wash this bitch pussy up off me, James thought to himself as he headed to the bathroom. He couldn't even look in the mirror when he walked past it. He can't *believe* that he really finna do this ho ass shit. He was just *disgusted* wit' himself as he cut the water on and got in the shower.

We cool and all, but I just-can't-do it. 40 years over some dope? Naw not me. That nigga built for that shit. Not me though, I ain't doin it. Fuck it. By the time everybody find out what I did I'll be ....

"Who dat? 'Mone, you back already.......What? You mus' wanna get in here wit' Daddy and get some mo' of this dick," he said, hearin' someone enter the hotel room.

"Naw nigga. Cut the water off and get yo' bitch ass up out the shower nigga."

"Hold up now, just hold up," James said, holdin' his palm out in front of him tryin' to buy some time. "H-how you get in here?" he asked, scared as fuck, 'bout to piss on the floor.

"Don't worry 'bout it nigga. Get out!"

"A'ight, a'ight, chill. I'm comin', damn."

"James Griffin. Ain't this a bitch? C.I. number 1147. You a ho ass nigga. Huhn, stick ya' self wit' that needle," the Snitch Killer said, tossin' James the syringe. "Don't ask no muh fuckin' questions. I'll blow yo *Got*-damn brains all over the shower," the killer said through gritted teeth. "Now inject yo' self bitch!"

I don't know what the fuck finna happen. I got a gun pointed at me. I ain't got no choice, he thought as he injected himself. Immediately shit got blurry, and his legs wobbled.....then he blacked out.......

CHAPTER 4

Nichole and R-Dubb's crib……

"Last night a Gary, Indiana man was murdered inside his hotel room at the Merrillville Inn, in Merrillville, Indiana. This is the second gruesome murder of this kind in 3 months. James Griffin, 31, was found on the bathroom floor by the mother of his child after she returned to the room with takeout food. His throat was cut from ear to ear, and the killer dropped a dime on his chest. Investigators further state the phrase "Speak No Evil" was written on the bathroom mirror in the victim's blood. The authorities have a suspect, but they say there is not enough evidence to make an arrest at this time. We'll report with updates as the story develops. This is Deborah Caldwell reporting live for WBN Channel 5."

"Uh Oh, looks like somebody eatin' pussy to-*nite*! What kind of ice cream you want me to bring home from work, strawberry or chocolate?" Nicole asked, laughin' as she changed the channel. "Damn, nigga didn't make it on the streets a day…….hold on nigga, where the fuck you go last night…….?"

CHAPTER 5

Later on that afternoon.......

"What it do nigga?"

"Who dis?" Chi-Murder responded.

"Dis R-Dubb. What up Vice Lord?"

"Nigga, you better quit playin' wit' me, you know I'm Folks. What's up? G.D. nigga!"

Dubb be fuckin' wit' him. Chi-Murder Folks to the core. You'd think the nigga bled dark blue. It's obvious the nigga from Chi-Town by his name. He a real ass nigga. Him and Dubb was in the same cell house for a while. Even though Dubb a Vice Lord, they clicked off the top.

"Ev'ry thang good wit you bruh?" Dubb asked.

"Shit, I'm just chillin'. I see ya appeal went through. That's what's up tho."

"Hell yeah, " Dubb responded.

"Ya' girl come pick you up?" Murder asked.

"Yep"

"I bet she did nigga. I told you, Shawty gonna merk yo' ass you fuck up nigga. She was ridin *too-tuff*! I did 'leven years nigga, and I *ain't never* seen nobody's girl ride out like baby girl was ridin' for you."

"You ever hear of a shot-gun weddin' nigga?"

"Her pops snap out on you?" Chi-Murder asked through a laugh.

"Hell naw, *she* did. She pulled a pistol on me and made me drive to the justice of the peace nigga."

"Ya'll wildin' out. I'm tellin' you nigga, a woman that loves you much as homegirl loves you will kill you. I'm happy for you. Just don't fuck it up. It'll be yo *ass,*" Murder said, still laughin'.

"Hell yeah, that's fo' real. But shit, on a another level, I know you getting' money out there nigga."

"Shit, what I tell you my nigga? I wasn't up in there frontin' like I wasn't finna sell no dope no mo'. I told you soon as I hit the bricks, I was getting them *bricks.* I'm countin' my lil' cheese up right *now* tryin' to get shit together. Shiiiiit," Murder said wit a lil' chuckle puttin' his hundreds in neat lil' stacks of 50.

"Fuck wit ya boy," Dubb said ready to do bid'ness.

"Nigga, I need some *weight.* You got like fo' of dem' thangs? It's hard out here, niggaz tryin' to tax me like 23. The S.A. over in East-Chi hittin' me for 85," Murder said disgusted at the drought.

"Just slide me 75 nigga, *aaand* the shit's all chunks, fish scales."

"Strait up?" Murder asked raisin' an eyebrow.

"Yep, I walked into a decent lil' plug. Real talk. It's all good," Dubb responded. "These is *reeeaal* bricks, lil' squares nigga."

"Bet! Nigga I can be over there in the 'G' in like a couple hours nigga."

"That's what's up. I'll be at the Merrillville Inn. Bring a sack-a-that kill you say ya'll be smokin' on up in the Chi." Dubb said.

"Fa' sho' folks. I'll hit you up when I get there" Murder said fuckin' wit Dubb on that set trippin' shit.

"A'ight then Self, Almighty," Dubb said as they started laughin' and hung up.

Hell yeah. All I need for bruh is twenty five stacks. Let me dip on over to the telly and hop on the phone. See how much of this shit I can get rid of befo' the wifey gets off work tonite, Dubb thought to himself. He was gettin' his plans together as he called a cab to the telly. *I'm finna hit up some of the niggaz I was locked up wit.* See, the joint ain't nuttin' but a social network of criminals. You meet a whole bunch of niggaz who do the same type of crimes you do, and Dubb was locked up wit' hundreds and hundreds of dope dealers makin' all kinds of connections. When you're confined to a small area, you able to observe people's character. Dubb knew befo' he got released who he'd fuck wit' on the streets and who he'd stay far the fuck away from.

CHAPTER 6

Task force headquarters……

"Damnitt!" Captain Jacobs shouted as he banged his fist on the table. "This is the second informant we've lost that was assigned to this Williams character. I know he's behind this shit. How the fuck does this keep happening!"

"What did you expect captain? Sanders was a known informant. Everybody knew he'd been workin' as a snitch. I'm surprised he lasted as long as he did. Hello? This is Gary, Indiana, the 'G', Gangsta Island. A snitch's life expectancy is no longer than your dick captain," Detective Susan Washington said as the other detectives bust out laughin'. Susan's a slim, dark skinned sista from Detroit. She's jazzy. She *still* keeps her hair in the tight lil' freeze curls chicks used to wear in the late 90's, and she sports ridiculously long air brushed nails. She wears big hoop earrings and carries louie bags. The bitch ghetto fabulous! The task force uses her to pose as a gold digger slash hood chick to get close to the ballers.

"And hell, the prosecutor's office basically spray pained the word 'snitch' on Griffin's forehead. How the fuck he just get out of jail all of a sudden with his charges dropped? I think there's too much pressure. The administration is rushin' us to bring Ryan Williams down. We haven't even given him time to break the law and we're all over him," Detective Smith said. "The administration is making fucked up decisions and blamin' us," the detective continued as the others agreed with him.

"Shit rolls down hill. I've got my orders and you got yours. No more fuck ups! We are to protect our informants," Jacobs said poundin' his fist on the table as his face turned red.

"Wilkins!"

"Yes sir cap'n," Bryan responded.

"I'm assigning you to our new informant, Jarvis Anderson, C.I. #1153. He's a Vice Lord out of the Bronx projects. He has ties to our target. Here's his file," Jacobs said tossin' it on the table. "Don't fuck this up."

"Alright cap'n. I'll take care of it."

"I'm done here, stay on task. I want Williams on drug and murder charges by the end of the month!" Jacobs said storming out of the meeting.

CHAPTER 7

The Merrillville Inn.....

"What's up self?" Dubb asked H.B. as he answered the phone. H.B. is a Vice Lord. Him and Dubb was in the joint together. The brother solid, always did good bid'ness. He never shorted nobody. He held his square down and treated ev'rybody wit' respect.

"All is well, who dis?" he asked.

"It's R-Dubb, bruh."

"Aw shit, for real? Where you at now? Last I heard you was in 'GC' cellhouse," H.B. said.

"I'm home bruh."

"For real? On what?" H.B. asked figurin' Dubb was bullshittin'.

"On the nation self, I'm home. I told ya'll I was gonna win that appeal. The shit was in the paper and ev'ry thang."

"Aw yeah? That's what's up. I know you tryin' to get some money and shit but it's fucked up out here right now. I can't even get on and shit. It's dry-n-a-bitch right now," H.B. said thinkin' Dubb needed some work.

"I can make it snow for ya bruh," Dubb said.

"Fa' sho'?"

"Sho nuff'," Dubb responded.

"Shit, I need like 2 of them thangs. Can you stand it?"

"Yep, I need 36."

"Quit bullshtttin! You mus' done hit a lick, niggaz is *taxin* right now," H.B. said happy wit' the ticket. He was ready to spend $42,000.00.

"Yeah, I came up on a lil' somethin'. Where you at? You still down there off 5th Ave and Buchannon?"

"Yep, but I'm out bustin' some moves," H. B. responded.

"Well shit, I'm at the Merrillville Inn room 208. Slide through when you get done."

"Fa' sho'. Gimme a few and I'll be there, Almighty."

"All is well," Dubb said then they hung up.......

Dubb sat back and caught a re-run of the "The Game" on B.E.T.. Halfway through the episode, there was a knock at the do'...........

"Who is it?" Dubb asked, raisin' up off the bed headed to answer it.

"It's me Folk."

Aw hell. I know that voice anywhere. That's Chi-Murder, he thought to himself.

"C'mon in Self," Dubb said openin' the do', lettin' Chi-

Murder in. As they exchanged hugs, Chi-Murder marked the letter "G" on Dubbs' back wit his fist. Dubb pushed Murder off him and they squared up and slap-boxed throwin' a couple blows at each other laughin' like homies do.

"Quit playin' nigga. Let's handle this bid'ness," Murder said smilin'-n-shit, throwin' 15 stacks of 5 thousand on the bed, and Dubb thumbed through em' real quick........

"My nigga," Dubb said handin' him a sack wit' fo' kilos in it. Strait piss, pearly white bricks, each one a solid chunk!

"Damn bruh, you wasn't playin' was you? Is there some mo' of this shit?" Murder asked checkin' one of the bricks out.

"I don't know, I'll let you know though, soon as I find out what's up," Dubb responded.

"A'ight my nigga. I'm finna jump back on the road, good lookin' out. We damn sho' gonna do mo' bid'ness."

"Fa' sho' my nigga," Dubb said as they exchanged hugs, then Murder turned and left......

"Knock-knock-knock. *Damn, who is it that quick?* Dubb asked hisself as he went to look through the peephole. *Aw shit, it's Murder,* Dubb said as he opened the do'.

"I almost fa'got. Here go the smoke you ast' fo', strait killa. I can get this shit all day an' day."

"A'ight my nigga," Dubb said takin' the sack as Murder turned and left. Then he went and sat down at the table and busted the sack open. Chi-Murder left him a half zip of some sticky shit. Dubb twisted up a Swisha and puffed on it while he looked at videos, thinkin' bout Nikki's sexy ass. *I'm gonna spoil that girl first chance I get. Baby girl really held me down. She ain't gotta worry 'bout me fuckin' wit none of these bitches. Wasn't none of these ho's around when I was locked up. The only one that was there was my sweet lil' Nichole and I'll never forget it.*

CHAPTER 8

Merrillville Methodist Hospital.......

"I ain't got all day to be fuckin' wit' you. I gotta tend to my hall. Else you want the shit or you don't," Nichole snapped on Dr. Robert Chandler, a pediatric surgeon at the hospital.

"Dammitt Nichole. Five thousand dollars for five ounces?" the doctor asked complaining 'bout the price.

"You got'damn right! This shit is pure. You gonna *have* to cut it. Shit, you a doctor, you know how to mix shit. You can put 100% cut on that shit and you'll have 10 ounces. That shit'll *still* be some fire ass nose candy. You can sell some to ya'll lil' doctor friends or whatever," she said knowin' it was the truth. A lot of doctors in the hospital like to snort, so they can stay up workin' those long shifts. They loved to spend. Ryan didn't know it, but she sold them a lil' powder on the side to help take care of him while he was in the joint.

"That's still kinda steep," the doctor replied, still complainin'.

"Well, you can always take ya' lil' pale ass on down to the projects and get some a lil' cheaper," Nichole said smilin', lookin' at the doctor like he's crazy. "Here, try some," she said openin' one of the ounces and choppin' the powder with a lil' blade lyin' on the desk. She set out a nice lil' line for him. "There, try it," she said as she backed away givin' him some room.......

"Shhhhhhhhnnnnnfff!" Was the sound of the doctor snortin' the long ass line Nikki cut out for him. "Mmmpf,

mmmpf......shhhnnf, shhhnnf," the doctor sniffed trying to clear his sinuses. Then he leaned back waitin' for it to kick in on his ass......

Oh my gosh, oh my gosh!" he said having trouble swallowing, grabbing at his throat as his heart started pumpin' faster and faster.

"What's wrong doc, you okay?" Nikki asked startin' to get a lil' nervous.

"I can't swallow," he said as he started touchin' his nose. "And, and, and I can't feel my nose! I can't .... my face, I can't feel it! Holy fuck! I've never, ooh fuck! I'll take the shit. I'll take it!" he said unlockin' his drawer going for his cash box. "I'll need some more tomorrow okay? I'll pay for it, thanks," the doctor said all jittery-n-shit as he hurriedly fumbled through the bills, throwin' five thousand dollars on the desk. Then Nurse Nichole Williams snatched the money off his desk and left the office headed to her hall to tend to all the lil' kids she takes care of on 4B.......

CHAPTER 9

Dubb was just sittin' in the hotel room gettin' high-n-a-bitch, smokin' on some of that killa' Murder left. He was gettin' his game plan together waitin' on H.B. when there was a knock at he do'......

Dubb walked over and looked at the peephole and sho' nuff, it's H.B.

"What's hap'nin bruh?" Dubb asked letting him in.

"Tryin' to get this money, feel me?"

"Fa' sho'," Dubb responded.

"Shiiiiit, where it's at?" the brother asked rubbin' his hands together ready to get down to bid'ness.

"Right here," Dubb said as he opened a dresser drawer and set 2 bricks on the table.

"Can I check em out?" H.B. asked.

"Go 'head check em out," Dubb responded, puffin' on a Swisha as H.B. picked up one of the packages and cut the corner open to inspect the work.

"Aw yeah, this the truth," he said tossin' a bag of money on the bed. "It's all there bruh," H.B. said as Dubb flipped through the bills......

"It's all good fam," Dubb said after he counted the money. He figured it was all there, but from a past experience, it's best to count the money while everybody's present. Sometimes the nigga coppin' the work miscounts. One time, Dubb was shorted a stack. The nigga really thought he gave Dubb all the money. He just miscounted. Homie thought Dubb was tryin' to play him out of a thousand dollars. They ended up fallin' out over the shit. So, now Dubb counts the money.

"I'm outta here brother. Hit me up so we can kick it-n-shit. Good to see you home man," H.B. said as they exchanged hugs. "Almighty"

"All is well," Dubb said as H.B. walked out the hotel room.

After the brother left, Dubb called his twin.....

"Yeah," Bryan answered.

"I got everything together for you," Dubb said as Bryan answered the phone.

"Meet me at the house," Bryan said then hung up.

That's what's up. I guess I'll call me a cab and head on over there, Dubb thought to hissself as he found the cab company's number in his cell phone.....

CHAPTER 10

Merrillville Methodist Hospital……

"Hello," Alexis answered.

"Whad up bitch!" Nichole greeted her homegirl.

"Hey gurl, how you doin'?" Alexis responded mockin' Wendy Wiliams.

"I'm good. Umm, ya'll ho's got my money?" Nichole asked as she nibbled at her lunch.

"Trick, you crazy! We got you. You got some more bitch?"

"Aaaand yoouu knooow iiit!" Nichole sung. Her hustle hand is piss. Alexis, Ayzia and Armani are sisters and they all work at the Club 10, the new strip club by the baseball stadium. She fronted them ho's 3 ounces a piece. They owe her 9 "G's". At first, they was trippin' off the price, but just like the doc, once they snorted a line of that shit, all complaints went out the window. It ain't nuttin' for them ho's to come up wit' that type of money overnight wit' all their tips, lap dances and trips to the V.I.P. lounge. Plus, ev'ry bitch that strip up in the club either snort, pop "x," or do both. Them ho's ate all that powder up like candy. Nichole can lock some shit down with these bitches on her team if she wants to and she knows it. She just never had the desire or a steady plug. Back when R-Dubb was in the joint Bryan used to look out and give her some powder or some x-pills here and there, and Alexis 'nem would make that shit *disappear!*

"Good bitch, that shit fire. Bring us the same thing when you get off work. Call me when you pullin' up and I'll run out back," Alexis said.

"A'ight, later bitch," Nichole said.

"Bye slut," Alexis responded as she laughed.

"Tramp," Nichole shot back.

"Gurl, you crazy, bye".

"Bye, bye," Nichole said hanging up the phone and finishing her lunch before her break was over.

Nichole and Alexis are tight as fuck. They grew up together from kindy' garden on up. They grew apart a lil' bit over the years due to their lives takin' different turns, but no matter what, they home girls for life.

CHAPTER 11

The trap house……

"What's up bruh?" Bryan said lettin' Dubb in the trap house.

"Gettin' this money. That's what's up. You ai'ight?" Dubb responded.

"Hell yeah I'm good. We 'bout to get it poppin' bruh. I hope you ready," Bryan responded as he gave his brother some dap.

"Aw, I'm ready," Dubb said handin' Bryan a duffel bag wit a 100 'G's' in it.

"Now that's what it do bruh. I just gave you that shit yesterday; but listen to this shit, you know that nigga Jarvis from the Bronx projects?"

"Yep," Dubb responded.

"That nigga signed on to wire up on you bruh. Stay away from that nigga. Watch him," Bryan said starin' his brother in the eyes. They're not identical twins. They look like night and day. Bryan's dark skinned wit' a tall, lean frame. Ryan's brown skinned and short wit' a stocky build. But still, when they look into each other's eyes, they see reflections of themselves and they both know…..

"What the fuck! They keep sendin' these mark ass niggaz after me. It's all good. I got somethin' for his *ass* though," Dubb said startin' to plot on the nigga.

"It's all good Dubb. We got a leg up on these bitches. Let's get this money. We family, nigga. I ain't gonna let shit happen to you. I'm in the position to look out for you now. We'll murder everything movin' before you go back to prison, and a lil' bit of money will make homicide write whatever I want 'em to in their reports."

"That's what's up," Dubb responded.

"Come on downstairs. Let me show you somethin'," Bryan said motionin' for Dubb to follow him down to the basement. He opened up a false wall and pulled out a couple big duffel bags. "Here you go Dubb. You got 5 twenty pound bricks of weed and a thousand x pills in this bag here," Bryan said as Dubb ran numbers through his head, already thinkin' about how he gonna get rid of that shit. "And here's 20 ki's in this bag. This shit don't cost me nuttin'. I just gotta spread a lil' hush money around and put some money back for Uncle Nookie. Just give me 125 'G's' and we strait," Bryan said.

"Hell yeah, that's love nigga. I'm finna lock shit down."

"Watch ya' self. Don't fuck wit' nobody outside my area. For real Dubb. I can protect you in my jurisdiction. I can't do shit for you nowhere else. There's some scales and shit in there too. Weigh out what you want. Keep the shit here or take it with you. However you wanna play it," Bryan said.

"That's what's up."

"Aw yeah, I got some keys for you," Bryan said tossin' Dubb a key chain. Some keys to a safe, some house keys, and keys for a Dodge. "From now on, you can just let ya'self in. You can drop the money in the safe and I'll have the work or whatever stashed behind the wall."

"That's what's up," Dubb said grabbin' 20 pounds of weed and the bag of x-pills, leaving the cocaine and the rest of the green behind for now.

"And check this out bruh," Bryan said motionin' Dubb over to a lil' work bench. When Dubb made it over to him, he opened up another duffel bag.... *Oh shit!* He thought to himself.

"You can't be out here naked nigga," Bryan said pattin' Dubb on the back.

"Damn nigga!" Dubb said pullin' the heat out the bag. Bryan gave him a glock 40 wit 2 clips and an old school Uzi wit' 4, 32 round clips. The *real* Uzi, it shoots 9 millimeter bullets, not no lil' 22's....shit! "I'm strait now".

"Let's go on back upstairs," Bryan said leadin' him up the steps.

"What these Dodge keys fo'?" Dubb asked as he followed in behind Bryan.

"Nuttin' really. I figured you needed somethin' to get around in so I got you a lil' Dodge from the chop-shop. It ain't nuttin' much. They owe me some favors. Feel me?" Bryan explained.

"Aw yeah?"

"Yep, you got everything?" he asked headin' to the side do' leadin' to the garage.

"Yeah, I got it all."

"C'mon on out to the garage," Bryan said holdin' the do' open……

"Hell naw! Damn bruh. This muh fucka cold! I thought you said it ain't nuttin much?" Dubb said as his twin brother sat there laughin', lovin' the expression on his face. "What's it sittin' on, 26's?"

"Naw, them 28's homie. Twenty-eight inch Divincci's--the real deal. They say 28's won't fit on a Magnum. Shiiiiit, there they go."

"Look at this paint! Eeeeewwweeee!" Bryan just gave him a pearl white 2010 Dodge Magnum wit' a chrome grill, sittin' on 28's. The paint pearl for real. I mean it's flaky. It glistens-n-shit, and you can see the lil' greenish, turquoise and purple rainbows in it." Damn 'B', I 'ont know what to say."

"Don't say nothin'. Throw that shit in the ride and get the fuck outta here. The garage opener is on the visor. Don't bust ya eardrums out nigga. You got 4 JL competition subs in the back wit 2, 2,500 watt JL competition amps pushin' 'em. It's loaded baby boy. You got 8, 8 inch mid-bass speakers, mids and Hi's and the amps to push 'em, crossovers and all that shit. That ride is ready for the show. Open the do'. You got off-white leather interior in there nigga. Wipe ya feet off before you get in."

Dubb hopped in the ride, sinkin' into the butter soft leather, awe-struck by the interior. It had a custom wood grain dash and steerin' wheel. He stuck the key in the ignition and started the ride. Dubb pushed the button on the garage do' opener and backed out the driveway. As he hit the power button on the disc player, the beats came through poundin', beatin' hard-n-a-bitch as he turned on to Indiana Street. Shit sound *good*! It's a mix tape full of rappers from the area like CCA, Ric Jilla, Freddie Gibbs, Slufoot, the Grind Family, Thugged Out, the MCG's and this bitch named See Saw. She off the chain! The mix tape raw. They snappin' over all the newest beats. A local producer from No Tamin Entertainment named Finga' Roll is hostin' it. *I better turn this shit down befo' I get pulled the fuck over*, Dubb thought to himself as he bent the corner headed to the jewelry sto'.

CHAPTER 12

Outside the strip club……

"I'm finna pull up out back. Bring yo' ass outside ho," Nichole said into her cell phone.

"Oh, okay," Alexis said, hangin' up and leavin' the strippers dressin' room. She's the club's number 1 money maker wit her sista's followin' close in behind her. She thick-n-a-muh-fucka. Ass so phat she can pick a Coke bottle right up off the floor wit her booty cheeks! Her and her sista's is black-a-neese, that's Black and Japanese mixed. They all got long silky jet black hair.

Her sista Ayzia a strait ho and she'll tell you that shit herself. Bitch got *game*. It's crazy though cause she's married. She got 8 kids by like 9-10 different niggaz. Yeah, a couple of em's paternity is in question. So, 'bout two of them babies is bein' claimed by more than one nigga. But, you have to respect the ho. She ain't ashamed to say her pussy pays the bills. Strait drama queen. She posts all her drama on Twitter as it unfolds. The funny thing is, she has followers and fans on that shit. People really log on to Twitter to see what's finna pop off wit' this bitch next. All it's gonna take is for the producers of VH1 to log on her page and the bitch gonna have a reality show.

Last but not least, Armani. She looks like her name. Baby girl is *beautiful*. She 'posed to be somebody's wife, not strippin' in nobody's strip club. She's just cursed. She got real bad luck wit' men. One nigga turned out to be gay. Another nigga got arrested. Turned out he was a child molester. Punk muh fucka got damn near life for playin' wit lil' girls and boys in 4 different states. She called the cops on her last nigga. He took off in her car after they got into a fight and he got killed in a high speed chase tryin' to get away. She lost it for a minute and had a nervous breakdown. She was walkin' around snorted the fuck out. But now she on top of her game. Won't no nigga her age fuck wit' her though. So she fuckin' wit' this 'lil high school nigga. He a young hoopstar. They say he goin' to the Pro's and Armani tryin' to go right wit' him. Every morning when she's done doin' private parties and strippin', she runs strait home to fuck the *shit* out the lil' nigga, fix him some pop-tarts and co-co puffs and take him to school. Kissin' him and givin' him lunch money like a good mommy should. Bottom line, these 3 ho's equal *money*!

"Hey gurl," Alexis said gettin' in the car.

"Bitch! What took you so long? You know better than to keep yo' pimp waitin'. You dig what I'm sayin' ho? See time is money and money is time. I'm tryin' to get it jiggalatin' out here bitch. You better get yo' mind right," Nichole said as she play slapped her, doin' her best pimp impression.

"I'm sorry daddy, I'm sorry," Alexis said holdin' her face, laughin' as she gave Nichole the 9 thousand dollars her and her sisters owe.

"Here you go girl. Ya'll doin' alright?" Nicole asked as she gave her 9 more ounces.

"Yeah, we good, but how *you* doin'?" Alexis asked in her Wendy Williams voice. "Look at you bitch, just look at you. Glowin-n-shit. You fuckin' whore! Done finally got you some dick and don't know how to act. *You* the ho. Bet you been fuckin' nonstop since Dubb got back ain't you?" Alexis said crackin' up.

"Yoouu knoooww iiiit!" Nichole sang blusin'.

"Five years, no dick? Guuurl I don't know how you did it. Couldn't 've been me. I know one thang, I hear *anything* about that nigga I'm cuttin' his dick off myself!"

"Watch it bitch, ain't *no* ho touchin' my man's dick," Nichole said laughin', but serious as hell.

"So ya'll got married huh?"

"Yep."

"Where's your ring? How you married and ain't got no ring?" Alexis asked hatin' on the low like most bitches do who ain't got no man.

"I'm gonna get one," Nicole said. She was embarrassed she don't have a ring, but at the same time she was feelin' like she didn't need one. This is because the bond she has wit' Ryan is stronger than any love she has ever seen between a couple, and it wasn't formed by no ring.

"It's finna be on gurl. We got this new white bitch named Candace. She calls herself Candy Cane. She gets rid of a lot of candy. That bitch a go-getter. Tomorrow I might need 12 ounces instead of 9," Alexis said.

"I got you, just call me," Nichole said as Alexis got out the car. Nikki relaxed in her seat and pulled off. She gotta make a stop by the store real quick to get some ice cream. Her husband has a debt to pay.

CHAPTER 13

Nichole and R-Dubb's crib.....

Ryan been sittin' at home for the last few hours gone off a x-pill, smokin' weed and drinkin' gin and juice. They say orange juice intensifies the x. Boy something is doin' *something*, cause he is fuuuuuccked *up*! Nigga horny as hell too. Dick hard-n-a-*bitch*! And, it won't-go-down. He keeps lookin' at the clock knowin' his wife'll be home any second. Her bathwater ready, he got the slow grooves on and he's in the mood for love.....

As Dubb heard the keys wigglin' in the lock, he rushed to the do' to greet his wife. Soon as she came in the house, she was swooped up in his arms welcomed by a big hard dick, and a deep lustful tongue kiss. He went to the do' butt ass naked, holdin' his wife tight, squeezing her ass and nibblin' on her neck.

"Damn!" Nichole said out of breath. "Hold on boy, wait. Let me put this bag in the freezer!" she said walkin' into the kitchen to put the ice cream away. When she turned around, she saw that Ryan was holdin' a gift box from Alderman's Jewelers in his left hand. She couldn't help but notice that fat white gold triple wedding band laced wit' diamonds on his finger. She knows that the bands represent their past, their present, and their future. Ryan just stood there smiling as she was frozen in place.......

"Go on girl, open it," he said, pushin' the red velvet box closer to her. Soon as she opened it, she cried as her heart was overcome wit joy and happiness while she was damn near blinded by the bling. It was a 3 carat trillion cut diamond set on a triple band matchin' her husband's. Each one of her bands were laced wit' diamonds too, totaling 6.5 carats of ice in her ring. "I love you mommi," Ryan said as he placed the ring on her finger. He held her face in the palms of his hands wiping her tears wit' his thumbs. "For real baby, til' death do us part. You are so beautiful. I know waitin' on me was hard at times, but you stayed by my side. You held me down and I'll never forget it," he said. Then he kissed her again. Nichole is truly beautiful. She looks exactly like a curvy version of Nia Long, except Nichole's smile is brighter and her eyes are more exotic, kinda Asian lookin'. Ryan feels so blessed to have her in his life.

"C'mere," he said, takin' her by the hand, leadin' her to the bathroom, still naked with his dick standin' out in front of him guidin' the way. Once they made it to the bathroom, he helped her take off all her clothes, then she got in the tub. The x got this nigga feelin' super sensual right now. He poured Nikki a glass of her favorite wine. He had a bottle of Arbor Mist sittin' on ice next to the tub. He washed her feet, rinsin' 'em off, kissin' and nibblin' on her toes while she giggled and sipped on her wine. Then he gave her a sexy foot massage cause he knows as a nurse she'd been on her feet all day. He took his time and washed every inch of her body, rubbin' and caressin' every curve, stoppin' to kiss her here and there......

"Oh shit," Nichole said as she finished her second glass of wine, passing it to Ryan for a refill. "I don't know who's it is, but there's a bad ass ride sittin' out front wit' some damn near monster truck rims on it. It got pearl paint and ery' thang, you see it?" Nichole asked looking at her ring.

"Aw girl, that's our shit," Ryan said nonchalantly handin' her another glass of wine.

"You bullshittin!" she said, lookin' at him wit' her mouth

wide open in disbelief.

"Nope," Dubb said as he continued to rub and touch all over her. The x got him on one.

"When, h- how did you get it?"

"My evil twin brother," Dubb laughed. "He gave it to me earlier today."

"Now *that's* what's up," Nikki said getting' out the tub reachin' for a towel. Still rollin' off the x-pill, Ryan couldn't keep his hands off her, he was kissin' all over her neck and her back. The lil' beads of water tasted like honey dew against her sweet skin. "Save it little boy," Nichole giggled and swatted at him. "You got some pussy lickin' to do, 'member our bet?" she asked as she played wit the nice chunk of ice on her finger.

"Mmm hmm, I don't have to lose no bet to lick ice cream off your pussy," Ryan said still tryin' to kiss her as she moved from the bathroom to the bedroom. The 'x' is makin' him feel the need to have somethin' in his mouth and his wife butt naked, wit 'lil drops of water drippin' off her sure looks good enough to satisfy his appetite.

"Now be a good 'lil boy and go get the ice cream out the freezer and get back in here and lick this pussy," Nichole said slappin' him on the ass as he left to get the ice cream. Ryan went to the kitchen and got the ice cream, chocolate syrup, and strawberries he bought earlier. He planned on eatin' her up tonite anyway. He hit repeat on the disc player and turned it up on the way back to the bedroom. The nigga rollin' like a muh-fucka and the music is soundin' so good to him right now. He went and laid down next to Nikki wit' his face close to her pretty 'lil kitty kat. He ran his hands all over her body, admiring her beauty, the softness of her skin, and the smell of her soap as he scooped ice cream right on the fatty part of her pussy.....

"Oooh it's cold!" she giggled, flinichin' a 'lil bit as he put the cold strawberry ice cream on her. Then, he sprinkled strawberries on her stomach up to her breast and drizzled chocolate syrup all over her nipples, down her stomach and on top of the scoop of strawberry ice cream that's beginning to melt from the heat of Nichole's hot pussy. Ryan took his time, teasin' her, lickin' and suckin' the syrup off her stomach, probin' his tongue in and out of her belly button as she twitched, giggled and moaned in pleasure.....

"Boy hurry up and lick that ice cream, it's meltin'. If you mess up my covers you getting' a whuppin," she said playfully slappin' her husband upside the head. The real reason is, he's been turnin' her on since she walked in the do', her kitty kat's purrin' and her clit's swollen. She can't wait to feel his lips all over her pussy. Ryan went down between her legs lickin' and suckin' on her inner thighs, turned on by the sight of the ice cream meltin', runnin down her pussy mixin' in wit the chocolate syrup and her sweet pussy juice. *Mmm, it looks delicious!* He said to himself as he took her left leg and cocked it up real high, lickin' her asshole. He moved his tongue in and out of her tight 'lil booty hole, lickin' and suckin' all the chocolate syrup and ice cream out of it as she shrieked in pleasure. Then he worked his way up, stickin' his tongue deep inside her tunnel. He moved it in and out of her pussy, navigatin' his tongue up and down her sweet, slippery canal. He flicked his tongue all over her clit as it's pulsatin' along wit' the beat of her heart, making her feel like she's 'bout to explode. Then, he buried his face deep in between her pussy lips as she gripped the back of his head.

"Oh, oh! Shit Dubb. I love you baby!" Nikki cried out in pleasure as her husband continued to devour the ice cream as it mixed in wit' her sweetness. His whole face got sticky as he feasted on the mixture of ice cream, chocolate syrup, and pussy juice. "Got *damn* you're a pussy eatin' muh fucka!" Nikki said out of breath as Dubb slid two fingers in her pussy while he licked and sucked on her clit aggressively, movin' his head in swirling motions as he finger fucked her......

"Aw yeah," Nikki sighed, out of breath as her heartbeat began to race as the pressure began to build up in her walls and her 'lil love button. "Hell ye-e-e-e-esss! I'm comin!" she said as her walls began to collapse around Dubb's fingers. "Hell yeah. I'm finna squirt all....over...your...fay-ay-ayce!" Nikki shrieked as she popped her pussy all over Ryan's fingers and face squirting her pussy cum all over his chin.

"That's what I'm talkin' 'bout, gotdamn you can eat some pussy," she said as Ryan got up movin' his dick up and down her pussy, teasin' her. Then he slid his dick in, slidin' it all in. Nice and slow. He gave her his full length, pullin' it all the way out except for the head then shovin' it all back in as he positioned himself on his knees wit' her legs cocked up on his shoulder. As he started strokin' her, they both grunted in pleasure. Dubb picked up the pace. Thrustin' in and out lookin' down watchin' her pussy swallow his dick. It looked like a set of juicy ass lips was givin' him head wit' a whole lot of spit while he watched Nikki's pussy lubricate his summer sausage. As he continued to pump in and out, he still has the urge to have something in his mouth. While Nikki's foot was all cocked up in the air, he eyed her nicely pedicured toes, painted a deep purple, lookin' like 'lil sugar plums. He grabbed her foot and took her big toe in his mouth and sucked it like a newborn suckin' a binky, takin' it out his mouth to lick and nibble on her other cute 'lil toes as he kept poundin' away givin her all his dick......

"Oh shit, I'm bout to cum *again*, oh shit," Nichole screamed as her whole body shook in spasms from another intense orgasm.

"Hell yeah, that's it mommi, cum for daddy. I love it when you cum," Ryan said as he continued dickin' her down. Soon as her body quit jerkin', he flipped her over and pulled her to him by her waist and entered her from behind.....

"Ew shit, damn nigga, you a beast," she said tryin' to catch her breath. "Fuck this pussy then," Nikki said as she put her face down and arched her ass up in the air to let him tap that coochie.

"Aw yeah, damn you a sexy bitch!" Ryan said slappin' his wife on the ass watchin' her booty jiggle as he hit her from the back. She got up on her hands and caught his rhythm, throwin' the pussy right back at him in a sexy grindin', windin' type motion grippin his dick wit her pussy....

"Oh shit, girl what you *do-in*, shit, AAAAAAAHH!" Dubb yelled as he came so hard his stomach cramped up. Then him and Nichole fell to the bed layin' there messy and sticky tryin' to catch their breath. They hopped in the shower and threw fresh sheets and blankets on the bed and talked about how each other's day went. Nikki was crackin' up as she told him how funny it was when the doctor couldn't feel his face when he tried some of that powder. And she told him how Alexis and 'nem snorted, slash sold all the powder she gave them as she reached in her purse and handed him the 14 G's she made today. Then Dubb told her about hookin' up wit the homie's he was locked up wit'. And she got shitty when he told her 'bout Jarvis bitch ass supposed to be settin' him up. Ryan's dick was *still* hard as Nichole drifted off to sleep in his arms. And about an hour later, Ryan was getting' restless from the x-pill and started poking her wit his dick……

"Boy you still hard?" Nikki said reaching behind her grabbin' his dick as she woke up.

"Yep."

"How long you been hard?" she asked as she still had her hand on it.

"Since like 8:00," he responded.

"Boyyy! It's like 2 in the morning, that's 6 hours! You better call the hospital!" Nikki said sittin' up reachin' for the phone. "You don't need to take no more of that shit."

"You been watchin' too many Viagra commercials. Shiiit, I ain't callin' nobody but another bitch if you don't sit ya pretty 'lil ass down on this muh fucka," Ryan joked as he stroked his shit.

"Don't get fucked up," Nichole said slappin' the shit out of him as she rolled over to slide down on it……

CHAPTER 14

The next day.......

"What's up nigga?" Dubb spoke into the receiver.

"Dubb? I heard you was out, what it do bruh?" Maniac asked. Maniac the nigga! He was in the joint getting it on wit' the tobacco. He a dark skinned heavy set nigga. Kinda put you in the mind of Beenie Segal from Roc-A-Fella Records. Homie Folks, he came up on 5th and Jackson. This 2010 fam, niggaz ain't on all that set trippin' shit. Money makes people come together.

"Shit, I'm just chillin' trynna lay low," Dubb responded.

"Yeah right. You ain't been home a good week and niggaz already talkin' 'bout R-Dubb the man."

"Who said that?" Dubb asked wonderin' who put his bid'ness out there like that.

"Naw, I'm just fuckin' wit' you. I bumped into H.B. outside J.J.'s over on Broadway. He told me you was out here makin it happen," Maniac explained.

"Aw shit, it's cool," Dubb said thinking to himself it's all good. They all used to rotate together in the joint. "Shiiiiit, I hear the whole city hungry. What ya'll niggaz need down there?" Dubb asked.

"Like 8 of 'em," Maniac responded.

"I need like a buck and a half, it's tight out here right

now."

"Shiiiit, I know it. You got some green?"

"Yeah, I got a 'lil bit," Dubb responded.

"Shit, what 40 of 'em run?"

"A quarter. I got some sponge bob's too."

"Sponge bob's?" he asked, never hearin' of these before.

"X nigga," Dubb replied.

"Aw shit, what the jar like?"

"Seven fifty, they the truth too. I took one last night."

"Cool, how we gonna do this?" Maniac asked.

"Just meet me at the Inn, I'm in room 312."

"Gimme a couple hours. I gotta get everybody's bread together."

"A'ight then bruh," Dubb said.

"One," Maniac said hangin' up, getting ready to halla at his crew to get everything together. Niggaz is ready to eat. It's been dry-n-a-bitch. And when a nigga do find some work a nigga want 23 a brick. 8 for 150? That's less than 19 a brick. That's love right now.

CHAPTER 15

Alexis' crib.....

"Girl, you need to clean all this shit up," Nichole said stepping over baby toys and packs of diapers-n-shit as Alexis let her in. By the look of the crib, you'd never figure 3 bad ass strippers live there.

"I ain't' cleanin' up a *muh* fuckin' thang. I'm sick of Ayzia and her muh fuckin' kids tearin' up the house. *Tired* of wipin' asses and pickin' up shitty diapers, 'lil bit just takes her diaper on off and runs around naked after she shits in it. 'Lil stankin ass. We fell out yesterday. I been thinking about movin in wit' my girl."

"Who?" Nichole asked not really surprised. She knew Alexis started experimentin' wit' girls after she started playin' wit' her nose and strippin'. That's when they drifted further apart.

"The new girl at the club I told you 'bout, Candy. I'll introduce ya'll one day. My sweet thang sleep right now," Alexis said sittin' down at the kitchen table lightin' a square.

"That bitch here right now?" Nichole asked raisin' her voice in disbelief.

"Yeah girl, now shhh! Fo' you wake up the whole house," Alexis said.

"I'm finna go see bitch, let me find out you up in here laid up wit' a ho," Nichole said laughin', headed for Alexis' bedroom as Alexis got up behind her laughin' and pullin' on her arm.

"Sit down, I'm gonna let you meet her, just not now. She's asleep. We had a rough night," Alexis said sittin' her back down at the table.

"Gimme my money dyke," Nichole said holdin' her hand out, shakin' her head trippin' off her homegirl. No matter what though, they bitches for life. Nichole just real like that.

Alexis counted out 15 'G's" and slid it across the kitchen table.

"There you go bitch, the nine we owe and half the money for the new batch," Alexis said.

"Whatever trick, ya'll bitches sellin' pussy. Ya'll ain't movin' this shit like that," Nichole said.

"I'm selling pussy too. I gets money bitch," Alexis responded. She got plans of leavin' the stripper life and going to one of those all black colleges down in Atlanta. She has dreams of bein' a psychologist. She wants to help people overcome their emotional baggage from fucked up childhoods. Nobody knows better than her. She was molested as a child and had an aspiring musician for a mother, who traveled the country in pursuit of fame. She never knew her daddy. The only memories she has of her father is some old pictures of him in her grandmother's house. The nigga got killed tryin' to rob a liquor store when she was a baby. So, her and her sisters were left to stay with relatives who didn't even want them in the first place. She's bout a year away from retiring from the strip club and if Nichole keep comin' wit' that fire ass powder; It'll only be a matter of months.

"Girl, what I'm gonna do with you?" Nichole asked as she reached in her giant knock-off Coach bag and laid 12 ounces of pure cocaine on the table.

"Unn Unh bitch, what's that on your hand?" Alexis asked eyein the 6.5 carats Ryan put on Nichole's hand last night.

"Hater! 'Told you I was getting one," Nichole said as she began to give Alexis all the intimate details of last night.....

CHAPTER 16

Task force headquarters.....

"Good job, Mr. Anderson is *still* alive. I can't believe you cluster fucks haven't managed to have him murdered yet," Captain Jacobs addressed the detectives wit sarcasm. "Wilkins!"

"Yes sir cap'n," Bryan responded.

"We still good to go on takin' Jamal Byrd down?"

"Yes sir, this Saturday. My squad is set to execute a tactical raid on his operation. We're intercepting his shipment. 200 kilos comin' down from Canada." Jamal Byrd is the big fish that's been supplyin' the area. His biggest distributor is Chico Ayala, a Spanish cat from East Chicago. Bryan been putting this shit together for a minute. He got 200 kilos of bullshit ready to make the switch. The real work'll never see the evidence room.

"Ms. Washington I presume your team will be raiding Mr. Byrd's residence then?" Captain Jacobs asked.

"Not exactly. We'll have surveillance on *him*. Soon as Wilkins' squad confirms they've seized his shipment, we'll take him wherever he's located. I've been workin' him for months. I'm takin' him down personally. The self absorbed, conceited son of a bitch really thinks I'm in love wit' him. I can't wait to see his face," Washington responded.

"Good job Washington. Here's your new assignment," Jacobs said throwin' the file in front of her wit' a picture of a sexy ass white bitch on the front. "Candace Cain, she goes by the stage name Candy Cane. She's a stripper. She works at the new strip club, Club 10. She's been feedin' us information for a while now. She's a credible informant. She's informed the local detectives that a stripper named Alexis has been dealin' a lot of nose candy inside the club."

"Okay, why do we give a rat's ass about a stripper sellin' a few lines inside a strip joint?" Detective Jarard Butler asked. He's the pretty boy, corporate type detective. He specializes in bringing down "upper-class" dope dealers. The kind who wear Prada suits and carry briefcases. Don't let him fool you. He getting his money on the side too. Him and Bryan watches each other's backs.

"We give a fuck because this whore Alexis gets the shit from Nichole Williams. Ryan Williams wife. That's why we give a fuck. If we can turn Alexis, we can get to Nichole. Once we get a hold of the broad and explain to her how long she'll be in Rockville's Women's Prison getting her carpet munched, she'll roll over on our target just like all the other wives and girlfriends."

"This might get a 'lil tricky. No offense to Detective Washington, but I think you should let me handle this informant," Bryan said, attempting to cover for his brother.

"Excuse me?" Washington chimed in. "I don't think you…."

"Absolutely not," Jacobs interrupted Detective Washington as she glared at Bryan. "This isn't open for discussion. I want Washington on Ms. Cane and that's that! Now go on out in the streets and make some busts," Captain Jacobs ordered as he gathered his paperwork dismissing the meeting. Detective Washington brushed past Wilkins rolling her eyes as she filtered out of the meeting behind the other detectives.

CHAPTER 17

The Merrillville Inn.....

"Man, what's *up* bruh! What it do?" Maniac asked comin' through the do', givin' Dubb a hug and a handshake.

"Just chillin' man, glad to be up out that bitch," Dubb responded shuttin' the do'.

"You *know* I feel you. I did twelve years up in that raggedy muh fucka," Maniac responded. It's a shame, the drug laws in Indiana are fucked up! This nigga caught a case when he was 18, *18*! For possession of 12 grams of cocaine. They gave this nigga 30 years. 30 muh fuckin' years! In Indiana, you do half the time, so wit time cuts he did 12. He spent all his twenties in the fuckin' joint. Ain't that a *bitch*?

"I hate the muh fuckin' police, well, most of 'em. This whole war on drugs shit is getting' out of hand. How they expect niggaz to eat out in this bitch?" Dubb said sittin' down at the table as Maniac tossed a bag of money in front of him. Dubb reached down and started countin' as they continued to talk.

"They don't, they want us to starve. It's all in they plan. They want half the niggaz on dope and the other half of us sellin' it. That way, half the hood is cracked out and the other half is locked up," Maniac responded.

"I feel you. That's why we gotta get this money and flip it into somethin' else. I ain't tryin' to be part of nobody's conspiracy or 'lil plan," Dubb said......

They continued to sit and converse while Dubb counted the

money. After he saw it was all there, Dubb gave him 8 bricks, 40 pounds of chop and a jar of (100) x-pills. After Maniac left, Dubb got a hold of Chi-Murder and sold him 8 more chickens for 140 G's. Then H.B. hit him up and came back through and copped 5 kilo's for 75 G's. Them niggaz is lovin' this shit. Ain't nobody came around dropping off pure un-cut cocaine in a while. You can take 5 bricks of that shit, turn it into 10 and it's *still* good. Dub thought about stretchin' it hisself, but why get greedy, he got $390,000 sum dollars, 2 kilos, 60 pounds and 899 x-pills....

"Hey sweetie, how you doin'?" Nichole asked as Dubb answered his cell phone.

"I'm good baby. What *you* been doin'?" Dubb asked his wife.

"Missin' you," she responded sweetly.

"Not like I been missin' you."

"You promise?" she asked.

"Yep."

"Hey, I need 4 of them 'lil thangs for work. I need 5 for the doctor. I only got one left and I gotta be there at 2."

"You ate yet?" Dubb asked her.

"No, I was 'bout to fix me a salad, why?"

"Don't. Meet me at Armondo's in an hour," Dubb said. Armondo's is an upscale Mexican restaurant. Dubb and Nikki used to eat there before he got locked up. It's where they went for their first date.

“Mmmmm, what’s the occasion?” she asked.

“You, us, our new life together, my freedom.”

“Awww, you so sweet. I love you.”

“I love you too,” Dubb responded kissin’ her through the phone.

“See you in an hour,” she kissed back.

“In an hour,” then they hung up.

CHAPTER 18

The Village shopping center.....

"That will be $1,853.95, and how will you be paying today?" the cashier asked Ryan as she rang up the pink and white Coach bag he just picked out for Nichole.

"Cash," Dubb said countin' out the exact amount, droppin' it on the counter as she eyed his knot.

"Mmm, lucky lady. I wish somebody loved *me* like that," the cashier said, flirtin' wit a sexy 'lil smile. She looked into his eyes as she put the money in the cash register and placed the purse in a gift sack.

"Yeah, I love my baby to death. That's my heart," Dubb shot right back at her to let homegirl know he's committed to his wife.

"Must be nice. She's very fortunate to have a man like you," she said writin' out the receipt and handin' him the bag. "Thanks, and you be sure to come back by."

"You're welcome," he said as he walked out the boutique with the receipt in his hand. When he got outside the plaza, he noticed the cashier wrote *Carmen, call me 219-555-8327* on the receipt. He just shook his head and threw it down. After all Nichole did for him, ain't a bitch in the world that could make him sway. Loyalty and respect are the rules Dubb lives by. He believes those are the most important elements in any relationship between a man and a woman, between bid'ness partners or between homeboys. Once someone violates loyalty, everything else falls. Nichole remained loyal to Dubb throughout the whole flick. Ain't no way he'd play her for *any* bitch and definitely not no gold diggin' tramp jockin' him just cause he paid cash for a $1,800 purse. *Bitches these days, boy I tell you.....*

"Hey Dubb! Dubb!" a familiar voice hollered out to him as he approached his Magnum. "Hey brother, what's up?"

At first R-Dubb didn't know who it was, but as ole' boy got closer, he saw who it was. *I know this bitch ass nigga ain't,* he said to himself shakin' his head.

"What's up baby? I heard you was home nigga. I been tryin' to get at'cha."

"Shit you ain't been tryin' to get at *me*," Dubb said twistin' his face at the nigga, turning to get in his ride.

"Damn, it's like that? This ya homeboy Jarvis. We go back. Hell. I heard you the MAN. I'm just tryin' to get down wit' you. All is well, Self," he said tryin' to play the unity card.

"Is all truly well bruh?" Dubb asked cockin' his head to the side like dogs do when they curious or sensing something's wrong.

"I mean, wh-what you mean?" Jarvis asked feelin' exposed, wonderin' if Dubb knows.

"What I *mean*? Shit you tell me what I mean. Bitch ass nigga," Dubb said grippin' the glock that's tucked in his pants.

"It's like that nigga, it's like that?" Jarvis raised his voice, purposely drawin' attention in hopes that he don't get shot the fuck up in the village parkin' lot. "Nigga fuck you nigga! Shit, I just wanted to get money wit you! I thought you might have somethin' for me," Jarvis continued to talk loud as more people were payin' attention.

"You don't *want* what I got for you. I'm a see that you get it though," Dubb said getting' in the ride, mad as fuck. He kept his composure though. He turned the key in the ignition and headed for Armondo's to have lunch wit' his wife.....

CHAPTER 19

Armondo's.....

"I hope it's alright. I already ordered for you," Nichole told Ryan as he leaned in to greet her wit a kiss.

"What you get me?" he asked takin' his seat, handin' her the gift bag.

"I ordered you some steak fajitas and I got me some seafood soft tacos smothered in lobster sauce," she said, ignoring the gift bag figurin' it's just 4 ounces of cocaine in there.

"Ain't you gonna peek in the bag?"

"Well, I thought it was um, you know," she responded.

"Open the bag," he said, ignorin' his cell phone vibratin' in his pocket.

"Oh, oh my gosh! I've been wantin' one of these *soo* bad. Thank you sweetie," she said leanin' over the table to give Ryan a kiss.

"Ya other 'lil package is *in* the purse," he said smilin' at his wife with pure unadulterated admiration.

"Oh, I almost forgot, I got your money too," she said, diggin' in her other purse.

"Unn unh Mommi, you keep it. Go spend that shit on whatever your sweet 'lil heart desires," Dubb said as the waitress brung their dishes. "I want you to have all the shit you gave up on while you was spendin' all your money to get me home."

"I don't know baby, don't we need to be savin' our money cause you *getting'* out the game nigga. I'm gonna help you get this money then we quit, and you gonna get those paralegal license, member?

"Yeah, baby, I remember. Soon as we get a couple million put up, we done," Ryan replied, fixin' his fajitas.

"You promise?" Nichole asked stickin' her fork into her seafood tacos.

"Yep."

"Pinky promise?" Nichole asked smiling, chewin' her food and holdin' up her pinky.

"Pinky promise," Ryan said lockin' pinkys wit' his wife. "That shit looks good baby, gimme a bite."

"Hunh," Nichole said holdin' a bite up to his mouth.

"Baby, you ain't gonna believe who tried to walk up to me like shit's sweet, talkin' 'bout he thought I had somethin' for 'em," Ryan said chewin' his food.

"Who?" she asked, still digging in.

"Jarvis bitch ass," he said, ignorin' his phone again.

"Aw hell naw."

"Yep, it's cool. I'll be to see the nigga though."

"Look baby, be careful. Fuck that nigga. You know he 'posed to set you up. Just don't fuck wit' him. And you cool. I ain't sacrifice five years of my life for you to come home, catch a murder case and go right back."

"I feel you. I'll be careful. He gotta go though baby."

They didn't talk about it no mo'. They sat and ate lunch, havin' a nice conversation. After they finished, Dubb walked Nichole to her car, kissing her deeply as he told her goodbye. She got in and headed to work. As Ryan walked to the Magnum, he checked his cell phone, 2 missed calls from Bryan.....

"Damn!" he expressed to himself after he tried to call him back twice. He couldn't get no answer. Bryan's phone must be off. It's goin' strait to voicemail.

Ryan hoped in the Magnum, turned the sounds up, and headed to the trap house to put his brother's money in the safe.

CHAPTER 20

Down in the Valley.....

Ryan was comin' down through the valley bangin "Clean Than a Muh Fucka" by Freddie Gibbs, a local rapper from G.I. who got signed to Young Jeezy. Finga' 'roll made the beat, he got a studio up on 40 somethin' and Broadway. Shit ridin too. ".....in a old school Buick ridin' clean than a muh fucka. Sumthin' sumthin' sumthin' wit' dem screens in the muh fucka," Dubb rapped along wit' the track noddin' his head to the beat. *There he go right there,* Dubb said to himself as he spotted J-Dogg and pulled to the curb. He was locked up wit J-Dogg too. Dogg calmed down the last half of his bit. He used to wild out. He'd stick a piece of steel off in a nigga in a minute. He did a 15 do 7 ½ for armed robbery and car jackin'. J-Dogg a Valley boy. They Vice Lords down here.....

"Almighty Self," Ryan greeted the brother.

"All is well," J-Dogg responded as his face lit up, happy to see R-Dubb. "You ridin' clean ain't you?"

"Aw shit, it's just a 'lil something, what's up fam-o?"

"Shit, chillin. Out here tryin' to move these 'lil packs," he replied, showin' R-Dubb a handful of grams in miniature zip lock baggies.

"Man, throw that 'lil bullshit down. I got something for you, hop in," R-Dubb said hittin' the locks. J-Dogg considered throwin 'em down, but he thought about it.....

"Shiiit, fuck that bruh, I ain't got it like that," he said hoppin' in the ride and shuttin' the do'.

"Yeah you do. How much dough you got on you?" R-Dubb asked as they pulled off.

"Like 13 hundred."

"Shit, so everything'll be even just gimme seven fifty."

"Huh?" J-Dogg asked him.

"Just trust me. I got a chicken for you, 10 pounds of chop and a jar of x-pills. I want $750 for the jar. Gimme 18 for the chick and 7 for the green. So, just slide me $750 and you owe me 25 'G's," Dubb explained.

"Aww," J-Dogg said reaching in his pocket countin out $750.

"Just reach in the back seat and grab that grocery sack."

"For real? Man that's *love* bruh. Good lookin'. For real Self. Niggaz been out here hurtin'," he said givin Dubb dap as he reached for the sack.

Not wantin' to be ridin' around the Valley "dirty," R-Dubb stopped by a trap house a couple blocks away. Him and J-Dogg sat in the ride catchin' up, talking 'bout coming up, maybe tryin' to start some type of bid'ness. After they smoked a couple Swisha's, R-Dubb left J-Dogg at the trap house to handle his bid'ness. Dubb bumped his sounds all the way to the crib. After he got out the ride, he noticed he had a couple missed calls from his brother. *Shit.* And just like earlier, when he called back, it went strait to voicemail. *What the fuck*?

CHAPTER 21

Nichole and R-Dubb's crib......

Fuck it Ryan shrugged to himself. It ain't shit else to do. After makin' call after call, Dubb was able to use Nichole's debit card to reserve a suite at the Embassy Suites in Downtown Indianapolis, due to a last minute cancellation.

It's Circle City Classic Weekend. Circle City Weekend is one of the biggest festive weekends for black folks in the country and it goes down in Indianapolis, Indiana. The event is so big that every room in the city is booked for the next year durin' the weekend. Tickets for the game is out of the question! Every year two black colleges bang it out on the football field. This year, it's Grambling State vs. Alabama A and M. The main attraction is the battle of the bands at half time.....

"Hey-ay," Nichole answered sweetly.

"What's up Mommi?"

"Nothin', just sittin' down for a few. I just got done makin' my rounds. All my children have been fed and medicated," Nichole said. Ryan loves that about her. She's really a sweetheart and she takes real good care of the kids in the pediatric ward of the hospital. She goes the extra mile, even stayin' past her shift without pay if one of the kids still needs tendin' to. She'll even sit and read, holdin' hands with kids who have whores and crackheads for mammas who don't seem to have the time to visit their children. She's gonna be a good mom. One day, her and Ryan plan to have kids of their own.

"Ain't none of the kids really sick or need any special

attention this weekend do they?" Dubb asked.

"Umm, no, why?"

"Good, you need to get home early tonite."

"Why?" Nichole asked.

"Why, why, why. Quite askin' so many questions girl," Ryan mocked her.

"I was wantin' to come home and spend some time with you anyway, what's your plans?"

"We goin' down to NAP for the weekend," Ryan responded.

"Oh shit, that's what's up! It's the Classic."

"Yep, we need to leave tonight," Ryan replied.

"Well, it's like 5 now. I can be done by 7, but I need to run by and see Alexis to make sure they strait for the weekend."

"I gotta make a run or two myself. I know what they need. I'll put it in the trunk for you. I'm gonna put 2 jars in there wit' it. Tax 'em 15 hundred for 'em, cool?"

"Yeess iiit iiiis," Nikki sang. "Let me get bizzy so I can get done mister," Nichole responded.

"I love you," Dubb told her.

"I love you too, byyyye."

"Bye baby," Ryan said, hangin' up.

CHAPTER 22

Later on 'bout 7:40 p.m.........

Soon as this nigga stops somewhere, he's dead-n-a-bitch, the Snitch Killer said following behind Jarvis's red, candy painted 88" Chevy SS. The Snitch Killer been tailin' Jarvis for the last 25 minutes or so waitin' on the perfect opportunity. It seems like the nigga runnin' 'round servin' packs. He keeps runnin' in and out of houses leavin' the SS runnin'. The Killer been following his pattern the last 25, 30 minutes. *Make one-mo-muh-fuckin' stop. I dare you,* was the thought that kept runnin' through the killer's twisted mind.......

Aw, hell yeah. This nigga's turning in the alley. I bet the ho ass nigga finna park the ride and run up in one of these cribs to drop something else off.

And sho' nuff, Jarvis got out the SS and left the engine runnin' as the Snitch Killer drove down the dark alley wit' the headlights off......

"Bitch! Don't *never* call me out to this muh fucka when you got short money!" Jarvis yelled punchin' the crackhead in the mouth in front of her children. He knocked her to the floor and threw her 'lil 35 dollars on the ground next to her. "It's fifty bitch!" he spat as he kicked her in the stomach.

"Don't hit *my mommy*!" one of the 'lil nappy headed niggaz said swingin' a wiffle ball bat at Jarvis in defense of his mother.

"No, Mar'quis! Get back! Mommy's okay," the crackhead said a little late as Jarvis reached back and slapped the shit out of the nigga. "You punk motherfucker, that's my baby!" the crackhead said rushin' Jarvis wit' the steak knife that was layin' on the raggedy ole' coffee table. She was able to cut Jarvis on the face before he slammed her to the ground poundin' her face like he thought he was Quinton "Rampage" Jackson in a UFC fight. Mar'quis got back up runnin' to his mother's rescue, followed by his older brother Mar'quan who had an iron skillet in his hand. Jarvis, still focused on the crackhead didn't even see it comin'. "Donk!" the 'lil nappy head fucker cracked him in the back of the head with the skillet knockin' him dizzy.

"Lil bastard!" Jarvis yelled slappin' the boy knockin' him halfway across the room. He got up, spit on the crackhead and staggered down the stairs from the 2nd story apartment. He was rubbin' his head tryin' to shake off the blow from the cast iron skillet. *Them lil niggaz got heart.* He thought to himself. That right there was prob'ly a turnin' point in them lil' niggaz lives. They gonna grow up to be dope dealers and gangstaz.....

Soon as Jarvis got in the whip, he felt a sharp pinch in the right side of his neck as the Snitch Killer rose up from the back seat. *What...they do to me up there? I know I ain't got no concussion.* He thought to himself as he blacked out. The last words he heard was..... "You snitch ass nigga."

CHAPTER 23

Alexis' crib.....

"I'm out front, come outside bitch," Nichole said into her cell phone receiver as she pulled up to the house.

"Gurl boo," Alexis said hangin' up, headin' outside...

"What's up girl?" Nicole asked, leanin' over to hug her homegirl as she got in the car.

"Shit," Alexis answered huggin' her back.

"I brung ya'll goodies. My hubby sent me wit' 18 instead of 12. We goin' down to the classic."

"That's cool. Here's the 6 we owe you and another 6. So we owe you 12 right?" Alexis asked handin' Nicole the money.

"Yep, and I got 2 hundred 'X' pills for you. You can have em'. Go 'head and get on. I'll look out since you my home girl. Be careful bitch. Dubb took one last night and fucked the *shit* out of me. Nigga's dick was hard damn near 8 hours."

"Eeeew!" Alexis said, jumpin' in her seat, laughin' and slappin' her girl a high five. "I know ya pussy hurt bitch," she said continuing to laugh.

"I been at work walkin' funny *all* day," Nikki responded laughin' wit' her.

"I knew it! You was walkin' funny when you came over this morning ho," Alexis said *still* laughin'. She's happy for her homegirl, but at the same time, she wishes she had somebody to call her own too.

"Get out my car ho. I gotta hit the highway," Nicole said jokingly but anxious to get home to get ready for her and her hubby's lil trip.

"Love you bitch," Alexis said, getting' out the car.

"Love you too hooka," Nicole said, puttin' the car in gear and pullin' out onto the street.

CHAPTER 24

Back at the Crib...

"C'mon girl, hurry up," Dubb called to the bathroom as he sat on the bed wit a XXL Magazine in his lap, rollin' up Swishas for the trip. Nigga beginnin' to "feel himself". He took the X-pill after he got home 15, 20 minutes ago....

"I'm comin' baby, gimme a minute," Nikki said getting' out the shower.

"You ain't gotta get all fly-n-shit. We just ridin' down to check into the telly tonight," Dubb said, lickin' the cigarillo puttin' the finishin' touches on the Swisha. "Just pack a outfit for tomorrow morning. We goin' shoppin' baby!" he said, bustin' down another Swisha.

"Aw yeah?" Nicole said as her eyes lit up.

"Oh yeah," Dubb responded. "Don't forget your lil' boom box so we can have some music in the room. Grab your CD's too baby," he said tryin' to make sure they got everything they need. He went by the liquor sto' to buy 3 fifths of Remy Martin VSOP, a case of Colt 45, 2 fifths of Arbor Mist, and a bottle of Nuvo. Dubb ain't trippin'. He takin' a gwap with him. He'll be able to buy whatever they need.

"Alright Daddy. I'm ready to go," Nicole said, dressed in a yellow and white velour sweat suit lookin' beautiful as usual.

"Let's hit it Mommi," Dubb said as they gathered their shit headin' for the do'. "You got your money?"

"Yep, like 43—no 42 thousand dollars. I put 3 in my checkin' account so there'd be money on my debit card," she answered.

"That's what's up. I used the debit card to book the suite for tonite, Saturday and Sunday. We gotta check out by noon Monday. It cost like $853 sum dollars."

"Damn, for 3 nights?" she asked as they headed out the door.

No sooner than they got everything in the ride, R-Dubb's phone vibrated on his hip....

"Yeah," Dubb answered.

"Damn nigga, where the fuck you been? I been tryin' to catch you all day!" Bryan snapped as Dubb started the ride, pullin' off.

"Hell, I been hittin' you back. Ya shit been goin' strait to voicemail nigga!" he spit back as he looked for traffic and pulled out onto the road. "Everything cool?" Dubb asked.

"Yeah and no."

"What you mean?"

"Shit, I got the bread you left. That's what's up bruh. You ain't bullshittin' are you?" Bryan said.

"I told you."

"What's up wit' Nikki? She been hustlin' at that new strip club ain't she?" Bryan asked.

"Yeah, why?"

"That's the information I got in the briefing today...."

"How the fuc....," Dubb interrupted.

"Just listen nigga," Bryan cut his brother back off. "They got this bitch named Candy Cane. She's an informant. She gave the whole play, how Nicole drops it off on Alexis and how Alexis is makin' it happen. They plan on tryin' to turn Alexis on Nicole then turn Nicole on you."

"They got the game fucked up. Lexis or Nicole ain't goin' for that shit."

"Goin' for what?" Nicole asked.

"Shhh," Dubb waved her off as he continued to drive and listen to his twin brother.

"So tell Nichole to back up off that club. She better tell her homegirl to watch out too."

"That's what's up bruh, good lookin'," Dubb responded.

"So what ya'll getting' into? Bryan asked.

"Shootin' down to the classic for the weekend."

"That's cool. Ya'll kids have a nice time ya hear?" Bryan said mockin' old folks. "Tell Nicole I said what's up, I gotta go."

"A'ight bruh," Dubb said hangin' up.

"What's wrong now?" Nicole asked, knowin' it's finna be some bullshit.

"There's a bitch named Candy...."

"Cane?" Nichole cut him off as she sighed thinkin' to herself *what the fuck*.

"How you know?" Dubb asked.

"Alexis been talkin' 'bout her lately. What's up with the bitch?"

"She's a snitch. She told the police how you been droppin' that soft off on Alexis," Dubb explained.

"Aw, hell naw. That bitch been talkin' to the police about *me*?" Nicole said getting' pissed off.

"Yep, done told the whole shit. They wanna use her to set Alexis up, then turn Alexis on you, then turn you against me," Dubb said, runnin' it all down to her.

"You damn right they got the game fucked up. I'm callin' Alexis right now," Nichole said, hittin' Alexis' number on speed dial.....

"Damn, this ho ain't answerin' the phone," Nichole said getting' impatient, tryin' the number again...."I don't know *what* this bitch doin'. She prob'ly up in the club. I'm callin' her tomorrow. Naw, fuck that! I'm finna leave this bitch a message," Nichole said, hittin' send on the phone...... "Hey girl, ya bitch Candy is shady. This important, so call me soon as you get this message," then she hung up.

"That's fucked up! Muh fuckaz gonna just keep on runnin' they muh fuckin' mouth."

"Oh my goodness!" Nichole said, gettin' upset, leanin' her head against the window. "Now bitches runnin' 'round here snitchin' on *me*? That's bullshit."

"I'm shitty too. Muh fuckas should be scared to tell somethin' the way shit been goin' down lately. But it's all good, we'll worry about that shit when we get home. For now? This weekend? We gonna have a nice time. Now fire one of those Swishas up and pop one of them 45's open," Dubb said, crackin' up to himself. Nikki beautiful. She's a very feminine woman, but she's hood. Some would call her "ghetto". She still likes to drink Colt 45. Now if that ain't "hood", what is? "Put some music on. I gotta catch up on all the shit I been missin' out on while I was gone." Right on cue, Nichole hit play on the disc player and "I'm so hood" by DJ Khaled came bangin' through the system.

....And they rode out, south on I65, getting' fucked up on the highway headed for nap....

CHAPTER 25

While Nichole was tryin' to call....

"Oh shit," Alexis said, sittin' on the edge of the dresser as Candy Cane licked her gently from her asshole up to her clit. Candy bad-n-a-bitch too. She got the face of Britney Spears wit' the body of Kim Kardashian. 'Lexis is sittin' up wit' her head tilted back in pleasure, teasin' herself, rubbin' her own titties while Candy eats her pussy....

"Oh Candy, lick it baby, lick it," Alexis instructed.

"Mmmm hmm, you like that bitch?" Candy asked, moaning, loving the way Alexis' pink lil' strawberry tastes.

"Uuuhh! Oooooh shit!" Alexis exclaimed as Candy inserted a G-spot vibrator into her wet and slippery opening. Candy spreaded Alexis' pussy lips wide open wit' her beautiful pink and white manicured nails and licked circles around Alexis' clit, flickin' her tongue around it, lickin' it all over wit' quick lizard like motions as she gently sucked it here and there.

"Oh my God!" Alexis said, bustin' one of her stripper moves, spreadin' herself wide open and placin' both her legs on the dresser in Chinese splits.

"Mmm, you taste so sweet Mami," Candace said, goin' to town on Alexis' juicy center. She was probin' the G-spot stimulator in and out of her fuck hole, watchin' it become immersed wit' Alexis' transparent pussy juice.

"Oh shit, you're gonna make me cum!" 'Lexis screamed as Candy's pussy was drippin' wit' it's own sweet serum. Candy reached down between her legs and dipped her middle finger into her sugar hole and stuck it into Alexis' mouth lettin' her taste her "Candy".

"Oh my God! Oh my God. Mmm, uuuuuhh!!" Alexis came as the taste of Candy's sweet pussy drove her over the edge. Candy took Alexis by the hand walkin' backwards, falling back on the bed. She pulled Alexis on top of her, rubbing her fingers through her hair. She was kissin' her deeply and explorin' Alexis mouth while Alexis caressed her body. Alexis moved her mouth down to Candy's perky tittie nipples. She was lickin' and suckin' them as she ran her index and middle fingers in and out of Candy's glossy pussy. She was using her thumb to stimulate her clit sparkin' a tinglin' sensation all through Candy's body, all the way down to her toes. It was makin' her break out in goose bumps.

"Oh Alexis," Candy cried as her wet slit burned with desire, twitchin' in hunger, wantin' to be filled. Not able to take it any longer, she pushed Alexis off her and reached under her bed and pulled out a huge, flexible 19" double ended dildo.

"Oh hell yeah," Alexis said in excitement as her own pussy hole began to tingle at the thought of the massive dildo glidin' in and out of her pussy. While Alexis stood on her knees, Candy guided part of the sex toy inside Alexis' pussy. Then she laid back openin' herself so Alexis could put the other end inside her wet, throbbin' pussy hole…

"Oh yes," they cried together as Alexis laid between Candy's legs sideways. They began to hump, rubbin' pussies as they shared the full length of the dildo, sliding it in and out of each other causing friction as both their pussies gushed wit' juice.

"Oh my good-ness, I'm comin' Candy! I'm comin', fuck!"

Alexis shrieked in pleasure.

"Meee tooooo, hell yeah...."

"AAAAAAGHH!!.......EEEEEEEEHH!" was the sound of them climaxin' together, screamin' in unison.

"Oh shit," Alexis said out of breath, layin' back on the bed.

"Tell me about it. Damn that was good," Candy agreed. They laid there and smoked a Swisher Sweet, kissin' each other and gossiping about the other ho's in the club. After about 25 or 30 minutes.....

"C'mon ho," Alexis said, slappin' Candy playfully on the ass. "Let's hit the showers. It's time to get money."

CHAPTER 26

Pullin in to Naptown.....

Damn, it feels good to be free, R-Dubb thought as him and his wife got off 65 takin' the downtown exit. Words can't describe how he's feelin' right now, rollin' into Naptown in a dope ass ride with the woman of his dreams by his side. "Wasted" by Gucci Mane and Plies pulsated through the whip shakin' the pavement. The song is perfectly describin' how they feelin' right now. They wasted! They both high as hell and drunk as fuck. He's soakin' it all in, lookin' at the city lights as he dips through the city. The X has him hypnotized by the illumination. *This is a million times better than bein' cooped in a 8x10 cell watchin' a 13 inch TV on a Friday night. This is livin!* He thought as he drove his Magnum into the parkin' garage.....

"You got everything Mommi?" Dubb asked as they grabbed their bags and the lil' portable stereo. "I'll come back and get the cooler later," he said, shuttin' the rear drivers' side door with his hip.

"Man, it's finna be on baby!" Nichole exclaimed as she hit the lobby button on the elevator.

They got off the elevator and checked in wit' no problems. The bellhop helped wit' their bags and showed them to their suite, which was immaculate. It had a livin' room with a balcony and 2 bathrooms. The master bathroom is connected to the bedroom, and it has a nice sized Jacuzzi. It had gold plated faucets and marble floors. After checkin' out the room, they decided to go to bed 'cause they got a long day ahead of them tomorrow. As they got situated in the bed, R-Dubb cut on the TV and it was tuned to the local news.....

"This is breaking news. There has been another body discovered in Gary, Indiana. The body of 29 year old Jarvis Anderson was found inside his red custom painted Chevy SS. His body was discovered in a dark alley near the Bronx projects which is notorious for violence. The investigation reveals that Anderson was involved in an unrelated scuffle just moments before his death. This is the 3rd of similar murders. The victim was found with his throat sliced. Leaving his signature, the killer dropped a dime in Mr. Anderson's lap as he sat lifeless behind the steering wheel and the phrase "Speak No Evil" was written in his own blood on the windshield of the vehicle. These murders are being investigated as serial killings. The murderer has been dubbed by the public as the 'Snitch Killer'. The authorities have confirmed that all of the victims were informants for the metropolitan joint task force in the Gary and Chicago area. The captain of the task force could not be reached for comment, and the authorities haven't released further details. As you can see behind me, they are still processing the scene. This is Kristina Herstein reporting live for WTHV 15 in Indianapolis. Back to the studio for more updates on the Circle City Classic."

"Heeell Naw," Dubb said as he looked at the TV.

"That's a damn shame. I hope this don't start no bullshit. Everybody who decides to tell on you comes up dead. You be careful baby, okay?" Nichole said as she tried Alexis' number again. "Shit, this skank *still* ain't answerin'!" Nikki said settin' her phone on the nightstand.

"C'mere," Ryan said pullin' her close to him, kissin' her on her neck and turnin' off the T.V.

"Boy, stop. I thought we had to get up so early."

"We do," Dubb said, turnin' her on her back, liftin' her t-shirt and fondlin' her titties.

"Mmm," Nichole moaned. Relaxin', rubbin' the back of his head as he sucked her nipples. Then he started plantin' tender kisses all over her stomach while he took her panties off. "Wha-what you doin?" Nikki asked as Dubb rubbed the tip of his dick up and down her pussy, teasin' her clit.

"Nothin......."

CHAPTER 27

At the Embassy Suites.....

"Mmmmm hello," Nichole moaned into her phone.

"What's wrong?" Alexis asked.

"You by yourself?" Nichole asked wakin' up.

"I'm in the bathroom. Candy's asleep."

"Look bitch, I need you to listen to me and trust me okay?" Nichole said.

"C'mon wit' it ho, what's wrong?"

"For real, you can't say nothin'," Nichole said.

"I won't. Now what's up?" Alexis asked, losin' her patience.

"Look, we got word from Bryan last night that your girl Candy's a snitch......."

"That bitch! Eeew, I'm gonna....." Alexis interrupted.

"You ain't gonna do *shit*! What you gonna do is act normal. You can't let the bitch know that you know. We can't run Bryan up. He'll lose his job. She just been feedin' 'em what lil' bit of info she *think* she know. She ain't wired up or nothin' so we ain't caught no cases. Just find an excuse to cut the bitch off. I ain't comin' around you while that ho around. Hell, the way shit been goin' down, the bitch won't be around long anyway. You hear about Jarvis?" Nichole asked.

"Yeah, we saw the news. I got you though, but that's fucked up. I liked her, you know. It's all good man. So what ya'll down there doin?" Alexis asked, tryin' not to show how upset she is about the news. She was really feelin' Candy.

"Me and my hubby 'finna go shoppin,' Nichole responded.

"Well, I guess I'll let you go. Have fun, bye biyaatch!" Alexis said as a tear fell from her face. *I'm gonna kill that bitch.* Alexis thought to herself as she balled her fist so tight her knuckles were white.

"Girl, you crazy, bye," Nichole said, laughin' as she hung up the phone.....

"Dubb baby, get up. It's time to get dressed," Nikki said, nudgin' him awake.

"I'm up boo boo, I'm up," Dubb said, sittin' up in the bed and comin' to his senses.

"I'm finna start us some bathwater," Nichole said getting' out the bed naked and lookin' sexy as hell.

It's gonna be a good day Dubb thought to himself as he sat up on the bed and fired up a Swisha. After he put the weed out, he brushed his teeth and got in the tub with his wife. They washed up and played in the water a lil' bit like kids, laughin' and havin' fun. It feels so good for them to finally be together. They waited five long years for this, and the newlyweds are going to enjoy themselves and have a ball this weekend. They got out the tub, got dressed and headed strait for the mall......

CHAPTER 28

The coffee shop.....

"Hey sweetie, glad you could make it," Bryan said as he rose to greet the pretty lady wit' a kiss.

"You know I wouldn't stand you up. I don't have much time though," Lisa said. She took her seat in the nice lil' coffee shop located on the east side of Chicago. She's a beautiful sista. She looks a lot like Beyonce', wit'out all the glamour. She was dressed in a pantsuit carrying a briefcase. They bumped into each other a few months ago outside the Cook County Jail. She introduced herself as Lisa Kelly, a criminal defense attorney who just relocated from Baltimore, Maryland.

"It's weird. We been goin' on lil' dates for a couple months now and I don't even know what blew you into the windy city."

"Well, I just wanted a fresh start. After all my business ended up all in the streets about my husband runnin' around with these different women, gettin' 2 of them pregnant. It was too embarrassing," she explained as the waitress approached to take their orders.

"What will you guys be having this morning?" the waitress asked as Bryan nodded his head motioning for Lisa to order first.

"I'll have a strawberry cream cheese bagel and a double caramel espresso, whipped cream wit' a shot of nitro."

"Hmm, I see *somebody's* trying to jumpstart their day,"

the waitress said wit' a smile taking down the order. "And you sir?"

"Let me have a chocolate coffee, extra sugar and two caramel rolls," Bryan ordered.

"Okay, I'll be back shortly," the waitress said turning to fill their orders.

"I'm sorry about the divorce. I'll try to make it better," Bryan said in a baby voice, smilin' as he kissed her hand.

"No, it's okay. I mean, it still hurts, but I'm getting over it. This is the easiest way, just start all over, you know?" Lisa said, turnin' away trying to mask her pain.

"You know, if you ever need a shoulder I'm here," Bryan said still holdin' her hand.

"Thanks," she responded.

"So when are you gonna start your practice?"

"I'm not, well not right now. I've been takin' my time. I've submitted a few resumes. I did good in the divorce. There's no hurry for me to get to work. Right now, I just want to meet people and get to know the city," Lisa explained.

"Here you go. Strawberry cream cheese bagel and a double caramel espresso with whipped cream and nitro. And sir, here's your chocolate coffee, extra sugar and two caramel rolls. Enjoy," the waitress said then hurried off to the next table.

"So tell me 'bout your job. Detective work must pay

pretty good for you to be pushin' a BMW 750," Lisa asked, bitin' her bagel.

"The job has it's perks," Bryan responded.

"I see."

"I'm a sergeant on the joint metropolitan task force. I'm highly undercover. I don't report to none of the precincts. Mainly, I blend in as a drug dealer, stolen vehicle dealer, or whatever and catch the big fish," Bryan explained.

"You have any family?"

"Not around here, no. My mom's people are from St. Louis. She passed away when I was in high school and I never knew my dad," Bryan said tellin' half the truth.

"Aw, I'm sorry to hear that," Lisa responded tapin' his hand.

"It's okay. My work keeps me busy. I don't have much time for anything else."

"Not even me?" Lisa asked flirtatiously.

"Oh, I'll make time for you sweet thang," he responded. Then they continued to chat for 20 minutes or so while they ate their breakfast.....

"Well, I gotta run. When can I see you again Mr. hotshot detective?" Lisa asked wipin' donut crumbs from Bryan's mouth wit' her napkin. "How about tonite?"

"I gotta work tonight baby. How about a nice Sunday

dinner?"

"We'll see," she said as she rose to leave.

Damn she's fine. I'm gonna make her my woman he thought to himself as he watched her strut out the coffee shop. He was really feelin' her.

CHAPTER 29

Meanwhile…..

Ryan and Nicole was runnin' up and down the Lafayette Square Mall dashin' in and out of stores like they won a million dollar shoppin' spree.

Nikki is really enjoyin' herself. She's catchin' up on all the shoppin' she missed out on over the last five years. Dubb told her like fabulous and the dream, "Just throw it in the bag." She gets to jack off the whole 40 G's this weekend. She done brought up a lot of J-Lo, Baby Phat, Roca wear and Sean jean just to name some. If she liked it, she bought it.

Dubb, on the other hand had just been chillin'. He copped a couple fits and a few pair of kicks. Mainly he just wants to see Nikki get everything she wants. His biggest purchase was a 40 inch chain. It was white gold wit' hella ice. After some debatin' and goin' back-n-forth he picked out an iced out Pyrex jar as a medallion. He also snatched up matchin' his and hers Cartier watches and bracelets for him and Nicole. He wants his wife to shine just like him or even better. All this shoppin' done made 'em both hungry, so they decided to grab somethin' to eat before they headed downtown to go shoppin' for Gucci and Louis Vuitton at the Circle Centre Mall, an upscale mall located in downtown Indianapolis.

CHAPTER 30

FBI Headquarters, Chicago office.....

"So what do we have thus far?" special agent in charge Dennis Montgomery asked Agent Locke.

"Well, so far I've found out that Bryan Wilkins is actually Bryan Williams. He's the paternal twin of Ryan Williams. Mr. Bryan moved to St. Louis and had his name changed while he was in middle school to hide his affiliation with the notorious Williams family. He's done a fine job makin' it appear that he's from St. Louis. His school records, college and all, say he's from St. Louis. He went to college at Ohio State where he was a silent partner in a drug ring. He was implicated by several informants, but no evidence was ever gathered to link him to the ring. After college, he graduated from the academy and worked on the South Bend Police Force here in Indiana where he climbed up the ranks. He was under investigation there as well. There were reports of drugs comin' up missin' from evidence, and during some of his arrests the drugs never even made it to evidence. He's very slippery. He's never been caught. And you do understand that he's a member of the Williams family, *Nookie* Williams, the infamous cop killer. He shot an off-duty police officer in broad daylight outside Willy's Pool Hall," Agent Locke reported.

"Do we have anything tying him to the murders of these informants?" Montgomery asked.

"Not at this time, no," the agent responded.

"Do we have any evidence of him leaking the names of the informants to his brother?" SAC Montgomery asked.

"No sir, and his phone is clean. I suspect he's using a prepaid cell phone to contact his brother."

"Well, keep digging. Get me *something*," Montgomery ordered, bangin' his fist on his desk.

"Do we need to inform his captain of our investigation?" Agent Locke asked.

"No. Not yet. That whole task force is under investigation. We don't know who's dirty or where the leak is coming from. We're not ruling anyone out at this time."

"So which one of the brothers do you believe to be responsible?"

"Both, I believe both of them are. I think they're working together or maybe even hiring someone."

"I'll stay on him. One mistake and he's ours," Agent Locke responded then hung up.

CHAPTER 31

Back in Naptown....

After they got done shoppin', Ryan and Nichole went out on the balcony of their suite and caught the last of the Circle City Classic parade. They enjoyed lookin' down at the large crowd and seein' the floats while they had some drinks. They sat around the hotel all day gettin' fucked up and listenin' to music. Then they went to Jilians for dinner and bowling. Jilians is a all-in-one date spot. It's classy, but you can have fun. You have a really nice restaurant on the first floor, and on the second floor you have an arcade and bowling alley. Upstairs on the 3rd floor there's a night club. They havin' a ball spendin' quality time wit' each other, kissin' and holdin' hands as people in the crowd couldn't help but notice the happy couple.....

Later on, 'bout 7:00 p.m....

It's nothin' but a car show on the streets of downtown Indianapolis. Niggaz got rims on *everything* from old school to new school, from Crown Vic's to Mercedes Benz's. Candy and custom paint is virtually drippin' all over the pavement!

Ryan was ready to show his shit off, so he pulled the Magnum out the garage and bent some corners with his wifey by his side. Niggaz had some heat down there. You could drive past some of them niggaz' rides and you could feel the bass from their cars shake yo' shit, like their subs were in yo' trunk. But when Dubb turned his shit up, he-shut-shit-down!

Later on that night 'bout 12:30 a.m....

"Damn baby, it's phat-n-a-bitch up in here," Dubb yelled

over the music inside the jam packed club. Ryan and Nicole looked so *good* together. Ryan had on a cream colored Gucci linen outfit wit' matchin' Gucci loafers. Blinged out! Ice drippin' all over the nigga as his Gucci shades hides his dilated pupils. X pill got him rollin'. Nichole is up in the club lookin' drop dead gorgeous in her brown Louis Vuitton skirt with matchin' blouse and jacket. She has on some tan knee high Louie boots, and she's carryin' a Louie bag. Her jewelry is just dazzling. They look like a celebrity couple finna hit the red carpet. They been at the club since 10 o'clock. You gotta get there early Classic weekend, ain't none of that showin' up at 1:30 a.m. thinkin' you finna stroll up in the club shit this weekend. They been dancin' and drinkin' all night. Nichole's kicked back restin' her feet as they relax in the V.I.P. lounge......

"You havin' a good time baby?" Nichole asked, leanin' over, kissin' Ryan on the neck.

"Hell yeah!"

"C'mon, let's go have a *real* good time," she said, takin' her man by the hand and leadin' him out the V.I.P. section......

"Where we goin'?" Ryan asked, curious where his wife is takin' him.

"Just come on," she said, leadin' him outside the club......

"Hey, hey, taxi, taxi!" she yelled, flaggin' the cabbie down. "C'mon, get in," Nichole said, hoppin' in the taxi.

"Where to?" the middle eastern cabbie asked.

"The Sunset Strip," Nichole ordered.

“The strip club?” Ryan asked.

“Yep.”

“Why you takin’ me to a strip club?” he asked, wonderin’ what’s finna happen as all kinds of possibilities ran though his head.

“Cause I want to,” Nikki responded.

CHAPTER 32

The Sting Operation……

"Team 1, this is team 2. We're trailin' behind the target vehicle, standin' by for green light," Detective Butler spoke into his walkie talkie.

"Team 2, stand by. Marked units are approaching. Wait for green," Team 1 leader Scott Johnson responded……

"Green, green light, go!" Detective Scott Johnson yelled into the walkie talkie as Detective Butler hit the gas drivin' his undercover Chevy Suburban right up to the bumper of the target vehicle as a combination of undercover and marked units cut it off from every direction…..

"Get your hands on the fuckin' steering wheel!......Let me see em!.......Get em' where I can see em!.......," various officers screamed in chorus as they approached the vehicle with their weapons drawn. Four other officers approached the vehicle, snatchin' the driver and the passenger out of the truck, throwin' them face down on the ground. Meanwhile, Detective Bryan Wilkins and Detective Butler pulled the tarp off the Ford 150 and verified there were 200 kilos of cocaine in the bed of the truck.

"This is Team 2. Take down squad come in," Bryan spoke into the walkie talkie.

"This is the take down squad," Susan Washington came over the radio.

"The eggs are in the nest. Take down your target," Bryan

said.

"Copy," Detective Washington said and began to initiate contact with Jamal Byrd.

"Alright everybody, let's clear it out. Get those suspects transported down to the precinct," Captain Jacobs barked as he walked around the scene.

Everything's goin' just as planned Bryan thought as he nodded to Detective Butler while he got in the F-150 to drive it to evidence. Butler followed close behind and soon as they got out of sight.....they made the switch.

CHAPTER 33

The Sunset Strip.....

Ryan and Nichole sat in a private booth inside the strip club. Nikki paid 200 bucks for their seats. They're just sittin' in the club, chillin', listenin' to the music, smokin' weed and drinkin' their drinks. It's some *bad* ass bitches up in the club. Sex is oozin' out of their pores as their hips roll and their booty's bounce to the beat of the music. Nichole took her panties off on the low and slid them in Dubb's shirt pocket as she leaned in to give him a lustful kiss, guidin' his hand down between her legs to feel her sweet moistness.

"*Damn* you wet," Dubb said as he played wit' her clit under the table, wondering where all this is goin'.

"Aw yeah," Nichole moaned as her pussy leaked more juice. The whole setting is arousing to her. A real sensual lookin' stripper named Star made eye contact wit' Nichole as she was bein' pleasured by Dubb's fingers. Dubb couldn't help but notice the two ladies eye each other as Nichole motioned for the sexy dancer to come to their table.....

"What can I do for you Mami?" the stripper leaned in whisperin' in Nikki's ear.

"We wanna see you dance," Nikki said, tuckin' 50 dollars in Star's g-string.

Bitch bad as fuck! She look just like Lauren London except her hair is brown wit' blonde and red highlights. She stepped out of her heels and climbed onto the large table givin' Dubb a good view of her pretty ass toes. Dubb's getting' turnt' the fuck on by all this shit as Star began to gyrate to the music.

"Take your fingers out my pussy and suck em'. I want you to taste my pussy," Nikki said, feelin' a mixture of jealousy and arousal as she unbuttoned Dubb's pants pullin' his dick out under the table, feelin' his pre-cum leak on her fingers. She looked him in the eyes as she took her fingers and sucked them clean of his clear and sticky juice. The stripper danced, poppin' her pussy, makin' her ass bounce to a sensual rhythm. Then she turned around on all fours and tooted her booty high in the air pullin' her g-string tight, givin' the horny couple a full view of her pretty light brown pussy lips. It looked like she had a lil' peach between her legs. Dubb damn near came right then and there as Nikki slapped her on the ass and stuck 20 dollars in her g-string.

"Unn unh," Nikki said, squeezin' Dubb's dick real tight as he reached for the stripper. "Don't touch. I just want you to watch," she said in his ear, then bit him on the neck flirtatiously, but wit' enough pressure for him to know she means bid'ness.

"You like that baby?" Nichole asked as Dubb shook his head yes. "You want Mommi to dance for you like that?" Nichole asked in his ear, hand still on his dick, strokin' it gently. Between his wife in his ear actin' like a wild and untamed kitten, and this sexy ass bitch flashin' her pussy on the table, Ryan feels like he's 'bout to erupt thick white lava all over the place any minute. Nikki pulled Star close to her and whispered somethin' in her ear. Then, Star got off the table and motioned for Nikki and Dubb to follow her. It felt like all eyes were on them as they made their way through the crowd trailin' behind the sexy stripper. Nikki gave her another 5 hundred dollars as they entered the private room. Ryan's heart is finna jump out his chest as he's anticipatin' some type of 3-way action. That's every man's fantasy. He's not really sure about him and his wife gettin' down wit' a stripper, but whatever happens, happens. He'll go wit' the flow. His mind's racin' as he wonders what's finna pop off but whatever it is, he's wit' it.....

"Sit down," Nichole instructed her husband, pushin' him down on the leather chair. Just when Dubb thought it was about to go down, Nikki motioned to Star and she stepped outside lockin' the door. Nikki's fantasy has always been to buy her man a lap dance then take him to the "champagne room" and fuck the shit out of him. Tonight she *livin'* it! Nikki removed her jacket and her blouse, dropping it on the floor seductively as she began to strip tease. Then she took off her bra slowly, enticing her man to the rhythm of the music, swayin' her hips back and forth, rollin' em' around and 'round, liftin' her skirt showin' her juicy pussy lips. She cocked her right foot up on the chair and spread herself open for Ryan to taste her river as it began to run down her leg. She's never been this wet and this turned on before. Soon as she got his face sticky, she backed up.....

"Get naked," she ordered as she dropped her skirt standin' in front of him butt naked except for her boots and her jewelry. Dubb damn near ripped his shirt off as Nichole got on the big leather chair, positioning her knees on the cushion and bracin' herself on the back of it while she arched her ass up in the air exposin' her gooey pussy lips. She's so wet and juicy right now.

"Arrggh!" Dubb growled as he entered her, grabbin' her by the waist, slidin' his shaft into her camel toe. Her pussy is so hot and wet. Ryan is lookin' down at himself catchin' glimpses of his dick in the strobe light gettin' nice and slimy as he runs it in and out of her.

"Oh shit, don't hold it daddy, let it go," Nichole said

knowin' he couldn't hold his nut from all the teasin' and temptin' she's put him through. And that was all he needed to hear……

"Oh shit, Nikki, gotdamn!" he growled as he exploded deep inside her wet gushy pussy. She immediately sat him down on the chair and licked from his balls all the way to the tip of his dick, tastin' and savorin' the flavor of their sex. She knows exactly what she's doin'. She lockin' her man down. She ain't no fool. She knows if she can't get freaky and fuck and suck the shit out her husband, there's some other nasty lil' bitch that will. So if another bitch pops up thinkin' she finna hop on her man's dick, she's gonna be a little bit too late. Nikki gonna already be down there talkin' 'bout *"naw, I'm cool, I got it."*

"Aw, I love you baby," Dubb said as his toes curled up and his eyes rolled into the back of his head.

"Mmmm hmmm," Nikki moaned as she continued to suck the hell out his dick, pullin' his skin back and nibblin' on the head. "I love you too," she said, lookin' up to see deep in his eyes. It's like she's in a trance. Then she got up and sat backwards on her man's dick, ridin' him good as her titties bounced up and down. She's aggressive on his dick too. She's been wantin' to fuck the shit out of him all night.

"Awww *shit*!" she said as she slid up and down on his dick, makin' sure to get all of it, not bein' able to take it no more. Dubb switched positions, settin' her in the chair. He spread her legs wide open, hangin' them over the arms of the chair as he got on his knees and pushed inside her. He stroked her wit' deep long strokes, movin' in and out in time to the beat blastin' through the club, long dickin' her as he played wit' her titties and rubbed her clit.

"Oh shit. I'm 'bout to cum! Oh baby, I love you, I'm 'bout to cum!" Nikki cried out as her sugar walls clenched Dubb's dick tight like a socket wrench, makin' them both climax, shootin' their fluids on one another.

"Damn girl," Dubb said, leanin' in kissin' his wife passionately. "That's the best pussy I *ever* had! Fuck!"

"Every time's the best time," she responded, touchin' his face, lookin' into his eyes while he was still inside her. "Now let's get out of here and get back to our room," Nichole said gettin' up so they could get themselves together.

CHAPTER 34

Sunday Afternoon.....

As they pulled into Gary, Dubb noticed they was bein' followed by the same car. It looks like detectives are in it. Every turn Dubb made, the car was right behind him.....

"Why you think they followin' us?" Nikki asked her husband, gettin' nervous.

"Shit, ain't no tellin'. Just a couple more blocks though, and we home," Dubb said, lookin' in the rearview mirror.

"UUUGH! I hope these bitches ain't on no bullshit," Nichole sighed as they turned onto their street.

"Look, when we stop, walk strait to the house. Okay boo boo? Leave everything in the car. We ain't lettin' 'em search shit," Dubb explained as he pulled into the driveway wit' the detectives pullin' in right behind him. Dubb cut the car off and him and Nichole got out the Magnum and headed strait for the house.....

"Williams, Ryan Williams. You need to come with us," one of the men said as they got out of their vehicle and approached the couple.

"For what? Who the fuck is you?" Dubb asked.

"Detective Robert Langley, homicide. You're wanted for questioning," the detective said, flashin' his badge.

"Call the lawyer baby. Everything'll be okay."

"Wh-why are ya'll takin' him? He ain't did nothin'," Nichole screamed as they put the cuffs on him.

"Ma'am, it's okay. It's just for questioning," the other detective said, tryin' to calm her down.

"It's okay baby. Just call the lawyer. I'll be cool," Dubb said, tryin' to calm his wife down. "I love you," Ryan called out to her as they put him in the car.

"I love you too," she yelled back as tears ran down her face. She is not tryin' to lose him to the system again.......

CHAPTER 35

Down at the station.....

"You're a real sick fuck, you know that? What's that now, 3 deaths you're responsible for, that we know about? Who'd you pay to kill Norman Sanders?" asked homicide Detective Craig Garner while R-Dubb just sat there lookin' at him like he's crazy.

"We know you killed Jarvis. We know all about your little altercation in the village parking lot. We got a dozen witnesses saying you threatened him. He don't want what you got for him. Is that what you said? Well, you don't want what we got for you pal. You better start talkin'."

Dubb just sat there silent, not sayin' shit. Not showin' the slightest hint of any emotion at all.....

"Make it easy on yourself. You're facing the death penalty here. If you work with us and tell us who's helpin' you, tell us who's tellin' you who the informants are, we might be able to get you parole in 20-25 years," Detective Drew McPherson chimed in, tryin' to play the "good cop" role.

"Fuck 'em Drew. Let him die! He deserves to die. He's a fuckin' serial killer, a sociopath, a drug dealer. He's a piece of shit. He's a coward, sneaking up on his victims. What, you're not man enough to face your victims like a man? Face to face. I mean you're so *gangsta* ain't you, homeboy?" Garner asked as he mocked Dubb, making lil' quotation marks with his fingers as he said the word "gangsta". "Why you punk out and sneak up on him? You sat in the back seat of Jarvis Anderson's car and slit his fuckin' throat, didn't you?" Detective Garner yelled, pointin' his finger in Dubb's face. "Why did you do it like a little bitch....."

Dubb just sat there, like he's been doin' for the last hour and a half goin' through this bullshit. Yawnin' and lookin' at the clock. He's kinda tired from the 4 hour drive from Indianapolis. The shit's kinda funny to 'em really. He done picked up on how the "bad cop" is attempting to appeal to his ego to get him to blurt out some type of confession in defense of his "gangsterism". He was just curious to see what they knew, and they know absolutely nothing! He's tired of this shit, playtime's over wit'.........

"Are you listening to me? Can you fuckin' hear? You're a coward, a punk! You're nothing but a low-life murdering son of a .....

"I want my lawyer," Dubb said, cuttin' the faggot ass detective off mid-sentence.

"What?" the detective said, pissed and caught off guard by the first words Dubb said since he's been in custody.

"I want my lawyer," Dubb said again.

"You do understand, that once a lawyer comes in here, all deals are off the table. Your lawyer is going to get involved, then the D.A.'s going to get involved. All that red-tape will be in the way and we won't have much of a say. Are you sure you want your lawyer? I mean, I think we can work this mess out. I understand pal. Nobody likes a snitch. I'd want some payback if somebody tried to rat me out," Detective McPherson said in a desperate attempt to keep the interrogation goin'. He knows that without a confession or some type of incriminating statement, they ain't got shit.

"*I-want-my-lawyer*. I've invoked my fifth amendment right, which means this interview is over. So why don't both you bitches get the fuck out my face?" Dubb said calmly, lookin' into their eyes with great confidence.

"Aaagh fuck it!" Garner said, wavin' his arms in the air as he turned to head out the door.

"You just made a mistake. A big mistake buddy. I can't help you now," Detective McPherson said, rising to leave the interrogation room.

This is some bullshit Dubb thought to himself as he sat in the cold interrogation room, wishin' he was at home with his wife. He knows they ain't got shit on him. But still, in the back of his mind, he's wondering, *"Am I ever gonna get out this bitch?"*

Meanwhile in the other room, you know where the other detectives watch the interrogation. The room they dumb asses think we don't know about.....

"That arrogant son of a bitch! He gave us nothin'. We tried everything. The bastard won't say *anything*," Detective Garner complained.

"He's good. He's a seasoned criminal. He knows we have nothing on him at this point. He understands that the only thing that can bring him down is *him*. Long as he keeps quiet, we can't do a damn thing to him," Detective McPherson responded.

"Cut him loose," Chief Bridges said walking through the door.

"What?" Garner responded gettin' pissed.

"You heard me. I said, turn him loose, let him go, set him free, release him. How many ways do I gotta fucking say it?"

"For what? So he can slit another informant's throat? We gotta be able to do *somethin'*. Can't we book him on suspicion?" Garner asked.

"Look, I want the guy bad as you do, but we have nothing right now. We're already pushin' it. I authorized you to question him. You didn't produce any results. His attorney called. We have to let him go. *Now!*" Chief Bridges said puttin' heavy emphasis on the word now. "Do you want the son of a bitch to win another appeal? Let him go!" the chief ordered, stormin' out of the room.

"Fuck!" Garner said, throwin' his paperwork across the room. "I *know* that bastard is guilty," Detective Garner said.

"Craig, just calm down bro. We just have to keep investigating. Soon as we get some evidence, we'll bring him down. But for now, we have to let him go," McPherson said, tryin' to get his partner to settle down.

"Fuck him. Let 'em sweat it out for a while. I'm goin' on break, you hungry?" Garner asked, leavin' the surveillance room.

"Shit yeah. I'm hungry," McPherson said, eager to go on break.

"Good, you're buyin'."

About an hour and a half later……

"You're free to go. But you mark my words, we *know* you're behind this shit and we're going to get you. Fuck up, just once, and you're going down," Detective Garner sneered as he held the door open for Dubb to leave. He got up from the table and left the station, not sayin' one muh fuckin' word. He walked up the street to the payphone and called Nichole to pick him up……

CHAPTER 36

Bertinelli's Steakhouse.....

"This is nice. I bet you bring all your women here," Lisa said as they were seated at their booth inside Bertinelli's Italian Steakhouse in Chicago.

"Actually, I've been wantin' to come here for a while now. I just hadn't met a classy enough lady to bring to this classy lil' restaurant," Bryan shot at her real quick.

"Boy stoppit," she said, laughin' his lil' line off.

"So, tell me more about yourself," Bryan said, lookin' in her eyes.

"What'chu wanna know?" Lisa asked, not sure where to begin or what to say.

"What type of woman are you?" Bryan asked her.

"What type of woman am I?"

"Yeah, how do you treat your man?"

"Oh, I spoil my man. I take care of him if he deserves it," she replied.

"Elaborate a lil' bit," Bryan asked, lookin' for a more definitive answer.

"I mean, I'll cook, I'll clean, I'll fix his lunch, and handle my…um…responsibilities in the bedroom….."

"Oh yeah?" Bryan interrupted raisin' an eyebrow.

"Oh yeah, but he has to deserve it, why? Do you wanna be my man?" Lisa asked flirtatiously, starin' him in the eye.

"Excuse me, is the lovely couple ready to order?" the waiter asked as he sat salad and breadsticks on the table.

"May I?" Bryan asked to see if it was okay for him to order for the both of them.

"Yes, you may," Lisa responded as she took a sip of her water.

"Do you like seafood?" he asked.

"Oh, I *love* it."

"Okay then, she'll have mezzelluna with shrimp and lobster sauce, and a lobster tail. And I'll have a t-bone steak, well but tender with a lobster tail, and we'll sip on a bottle of your best wine," Bryan ordered for them as the waiter removed their menus.

"Very well sir, your order will be here shortly, and I'll be right back with your wine."

"Now, where were we?" Bryan asked, forgetting where they left off.

"I was asking, did you want to be my man?" she responded, making eye contact as she took a bite into her breadstick.

"Are you ready to have a man? I mean, is it too soon for you?"

"You can't answer a question with a question." She responded with her perfect lil' smile.

"I'd *love* to be your man. I just didn't want to rush you. I didn't know if you were seeing other people or not."

"I'm not the dating type. I was married for 8 years, and I was with my husband for 4 years before we got married. I don't want to get out there on the dating scene. I'm more of a commitment type woman," she responded.

"Here you guys go. I'll be back with your meals shortly," the waiter said, bringing the wine and a couple wine glasses to the table and leaving.

"Are you a commitment type man?" she asked, continuing their conversation.

"You know, I've never been in a serious relationship. I wouldn't know how to act," he responded.

"That's because you hadn't met the right woman. I could be good for you."

"You could huh?"

"Oh yes, I could......"

They continued to have their discussion as the waiter brung their dinner. They ate over a nice conversation talking about their dreams, their goals, and their future together. They're a couple now. Bryan is really feelin' this woman. He's at that point in his life where he's been thinkin' about settling down, and she a lawyer too? Oh *yeah!* Because he's wrapped up in his work, posing as a dope man 24/7, he's only used to attracting chicken heads with no goals or dreams. Lisa wants to start her own private practice as a defense attorney after she makes a name for herself out here in Chicago. They even discussed the possibilities of them teaming up, with Bryan working with her as an investigator. Then he can quit all this bullshit police work. He's considering callin' it quits after Dubb pays him 1.5 million for the 200 kilos of cocaine he just stole last night.

CHAPTER 37

Meanwhile……

"……..I'm just so glad they ain't lock your ass up. I had a damn panic attack. I'm *not* tryin' to lose you. We ain't gonna have no peace around here. We gotta move," Nicole said, just wantin' to get away from all the bullshit. Lake County crooked as fuck. They're not gonna rest until they put her man back in prison and she knows it.

"Where you wanna move to baby?" Dubb asked as he smoked his Swisha tryin' to calm his nerves.

"I don't care. Anywhere but here. Let's just get our lil' money together and get the fuck up out this bitch," she said as her phone rang…..

"Hello," she snapped as she answered.

"Damn bitch, what's wrong with you?" Alexis asked.

"Aw, nothin'. Police fuckin' wit' my man, that's all," Nichole responded sarcastically.

"What happened?"

"Soon as we got back in town, a detective car started followin' us and *soon* as we pulled up in the driveway, them bitches pulled in right behind us. They took Ryan downtown for questionin' about them snitch killer murders."

"Girl shud up," Alexis said in disbelief. "Did they keep him?" she asked concerned.

"Naw, he here. But I'm sick of this shit already. We finna get the fuck up outta here. This ain't gonna cut it."

"Ya'll should go down to the ATL shawty," Alexis said, imitatin' the way ALTiens talk.

"I don't know where we goin', but we goin' somewhere. So where's that bitch of yours at?"

"I shook her. She came up a lil' short on the money. I saw that as the perfect opportunity to cut her off. I started a big fight over it, blew it all out of proportion-n-shit. I told the bitch I'ma beat her ass she come back to work. Ho started cryin'-n-shit, talkin' 'bout she all in love wit' me. Lyin'-n-shit, knowin' she tryin' to get me locked up. I don't know how niggaz do it. Ho's is scandalous and too much drama. I'm through wit' bitches, it's strictly dickly from here on out."

"Bitch, you fried!" Nicole said, crackin' the fuck up.

"Quit laughin', that shit ain't funny ho."

"Yeah it is," Nichole said, still laughin' in her ear.

"Anyways.......I got your money bitch. You comin' through or what cause I need some mo'!"

"Shit, I don't know. Hold on," she said, then covered the phone. "Hey baby, how much I got left?" she asked Dubb.

"Umm, you should have like 14 zips. Yeah, you got 14. I weighed it all out in ounces when I sent the half to 'Lexis 'nem and you took 4 to work, 'member? Yep, 14," Dubb said, thinkin' about it.

"Yeah, I'll be there," Nichole said.

"I need a couple jars bitch. That X is off the chain, and hurry up. 'Been waitin' on yo' ass all day."

"I'm comin' bitch. I'm comin', bye!" Nichole said, pressin' end on her cell phone. "I'll be back baby. I'm goin' past Alexis' house. They need 2 jars too."

"A'ight," Dubb said, getting' off the couch to go get everything for her.....

"Here you go Mommi, hurry back. I might step out and get somethin' to eat, you hungry?" Dubb asked, handin' her the package.

"Yeah, I want some fish steaks and shrimp from J.J.'s," she said.

"Sounds good. I got you," he said, kissin' her as she turned and left.

CHAPTER 38

Candy Cane.....

"Fuck!" Candace yelled out loud to no one in particular as she rolled over puttin' the pillow over her head. She hasn't been able to get any sleep. Too many thoughts runnin' through her head. She's paranoid. She thinks the snitch killer is gonna suddenly appear in her bedroom like the boogeyman. Plus, she's heartbroken over her and Alexis' breakup. She feels like one of those undercover agents in the T.V. shows that fell in love wit' their targets. She was really attracted to Alexis and had some strong feelins for her regardless of the fact she gave up a lil' information on her here and there. She never meant to hurt her. They said they wasn't interested in Alexis. The detectives said they wanted the broad who Alexis was getting' the shit from. *That damn cat*! Candace said to herself as she heard what sounded like dishes clangin' down stairs. *Won't stay off the fucking counters*! She thought to herself as she pounded her bed. She went to the window and felt relieved to see the undercover unit still parked across the street. She's felt safer since they've assigned detectives to watch the house around the clock. *Ain't this a bitch? Worthless son-of-a-gun is asleep!* She said to herself, seein' the cop sittin' with his head tilted back against the headrest. She still felt comforted somewhat, just from the sight of the car as she left her bedroom and headed for the stairs.

"Skreeeech, skreeeech, skreeeech........... Skreeeech, skreeeech, skreeeech...." Was the sound she heard from the top of the staircase. It almost sounds like somebody's scrapin' their nails or somethin' across a chalkboard but not as annoying.

"Skreeeech, skreeeech, skreeeech...... skreeeech, skreeeech, skreeeech," her heart is poundin' harder and harder wit' every step to the point she can hear her own heartbeat in between the sound...

"Skreeeech, skreeeech, skreeeech..... skreeeech, skreeeech, skreeeech." Her heart is beating faster and faster as her breath quickens with every step. Her instinct is tellin' her to run upstairs, lock herself in the bedroom and dial 911, but her curiosity is compellin' her, takin' control of her feet, carryin' her down the stairs one step at a time.

Soon as she reached the bottom of the stairs and turned into the kitchen.....

"Wraaaang!" the cat shrieked as it jumped from the kitchen sink and leaped into Candy's arms.

"Whis-kers!.... Whew." Candy sighed in relief, happy to see it's just her cat Mr. Whiskers. "Bad boy, you scared me," Candy spoke to the cat in baby talk as she stroked him across the head kissin' him. "Goodness gracious," she said truly relieved. Mr. Whiskers was standin' on the sink scrapin' the window with his claws.

"What was you lookin' at Mr. Baddy, huh bad boy?" she asked as she approached the window....

"AAAAAAgh!!!" she screamed, droppin' the cat as she looked out the window. She saw the lifeless body of the detective sittin' in the car across the street with the top of his head blown off. As she turned to run, there the killer stood.....

"Don't worry about him," the snitch killer said, pointin' a silenced P.K. Walter right in Candy's face. "Shut the fuck up!

Say one more fuckin' word and you're gonna be missin' your top too. You know what it is, you snitchin' lil' bitch! You picked the wrong people to tell on. Hunh, stick yourself!" the snitch killer ordered, tossin' her the syringe.

"You're gonna kill me. I ca-aa-n't. I can't do it," Candace cried, fallin' to the floor.

"Listen here you lil' bitch. Take your pick. Else you can have a nice open casket funeral or I'll blow ya muh fuckin' shit off and they can keep the bitch closed."

"I can't," Candy cried. "Please no, don't kill me!"

"Have it your way," the snitch killer said, shootin' the bitch dead in her muh fuckin' face. *Shit ain't always gonna go as planned*. The killer thought going to work, slicin' the scandalous bitch's throat.

CHAPTER 39

Nichole and R-Dubb's crib.....

Ryan and Nichole pulled up to the house at the same time. Laughin' at each other, tootin' their horns. Ryan was just gettin' back from JJ's and Nichole just got back from droppin' the package off and pickin' up her money from Alexis.

"What's up baby?" Ryan asked as they approached the do'.

"Hey," Nikki responded, stickin' her key in the lock letting them in. "What all you get?" She asked as they walked through the do'.

"Some of everything. I got some chicken wings, fish steaks and shrimp, some fries and a half loaf of bread," Dubb responded.

"Mmm, somebody hungry."

"Hell yeah, I'm finna crash that shit soon as I get out the shower," he said, puttin' the food in the kitchen.

"You need Mommi to come in there and help you wash your pee pee?" Nichole asked in baby talk, walkin' up to Dubb, kissin' him on the lips.

"Mmm Hmm," Dubb replied, noddin' his head, wit' his lips poked out like a lil' boy.....

They took a nice sensual shower together, washin' one another, touchin' and kissin' each other. This led to Nichole bendin' over, bracin' herself, and holdin' onto the faucets while Dubb entered her from behind. He slid in slowly, givin' her long deep strokes as he grabbed her soft, round booty cheeks, spreadin' her open, enjoyin' the sight of his big dick plungin' in and out of Nikki's pussy hole.

After their shower, they feasted on the large foil pan of fried food, hot sauce, bread and peach pop. When they finished, they laid in bed and watched their favorite movie 'Boys in the Hood' while they snuggled and held hands makin' plans for the future until they fell asleep....

6:12 a.m.....

On her way back from the bathroom, the news caught Nichole's attention.....

"Ryan baby, get up, get up. Look at this shit," Nichole said, wakin' him up.

"Huh? Girl what?" Dubb said as he rolled over. "Awww shit......."

"The notorious snitch killer has struck again, this time murdering undercover Detective Christopher Barnhill. Detective Barnhill was providing protective custody over confidential informant Candace Cain. He was part of a detail that was conducting 24 hour surveillance outside her home. Authorities say Detective Barnhill failed to check in. After several unsuccessful attempts to reach him by radio and cell phone, detectives became suspicious. Upon arriving at the scene, they discovered the detective suffered from a single gunshot wound. The coroner reported that Barnhill was shot under the chin at pointblank range with the bullet exiting through the top of his head. The informant, a 27 year old exotic dancer, had been murdered in the same morbid style as the other victims except she was shot in the head. The medical examiner report states Ms. Cain's throat was cut post mortem. The killer left his calling card by dropping a dime on the victim's chest and sprawling the phrase 'speak no evil' across the refrigerator. The investigators would not make any further comments. We'll report more as this story progresses. This is Deborah Caldwell reporting breaking news, live WBN Channel 5.

"Hell yeah! That's what the fuck they muh fuckin' asses get, now go to sleep boo boo," Dubb said, rollin' over, pullin' the covers over his head.

CHAPTER 40

Bryan's crib.....

"Yeah," Bryan said, answerin' his phone, lookin' over seein' that Lisa's sleepin' peacefully.

"What's up bruh?" Ryan greeted his twin.

"The heat's gonna come down, you see the news?" Bryan said.

"Yeah, Nichole woke me up early this morning to see it," Dubb responded.

"Shit's crazy, you a muh fucka wit' yo' shit," Bryan laughed.

"What you mean?" Dubb replied wit' a lil' smirk.

"Look bruh, we ain't gonna talk about all that right now. Main thang is gettin' this money. I got 200 of them thangs for you. I need 1.5 million and we're done."

"Aw yeah?" R-Dubb asked.

"Hell yeah, everything went smooth Saturday night. You know where it's at, same spot.

"That's what's up," Dubb said, gettin' excited.

"How long you think it'll take you?" Bryan asked ready to get this shit over with and quit the police force.

"I don't know bruh, a week, maybe 10 days. All depends. Shiiiit, I need you to keep homicide off my ass so I can move. I got questioned yesterday."

"I heard. They ain't got nuttin' on you right now, they just fishin'," Bryan responded. "I ain't gonna let *nothin'* happen to you. Don't worry 'bout none of these snitches or none of that shit," Bryan continued as Lisa stirred in her sleep.

"That's cool, just keep them bitches off me for 2 more weeks."

"I got you bruh, I got you," Bryan responded.

"Well shit. Let me get up off here so I can get bizzy. I been gone all weekend and niggaz need me right now," Dubb responded.

"A'ight then bruh, one," Bryan said, getting' ready to hang up.

"Oh shit, I almost fa'got. I wanna get Nikki a ride man. She been hangin' on to that Aurora for a minute, puttin' off getting' a new ride, tryin' to pay my lawyers and shit," Dubb said.

"Shit. Roberto 'them got a black 2009 Chevy Camaro they tryin' to get rid of right now. Cold-n-a-bitch! Chrome Lexani grill wit' a Lexani body kit, the rear end is flared out, and the rear wheels is fatter than the front ones. It's sittin' on 24 inch Diablo's. It's clean bruh. I be lettin' 'em slide. They always owe me favors. I can get it for you for like, umm 35 G's. Sounds and all," Bryan said.

"Hook it up. She gonna *love* that shit!" Dubb said, not

able to wait to see the expression on Nikki's face.

"I got you. You know I'm gonna look out for my family. But I gotta go bruh, gotta get ready for work," Bryan said, tryin' to rush off the phone.

"A'ight bruh," Dubb responded.

"Later," Bryan said, hangin' up, getting' out the bed, headin' for the shower.

"I thought you didn't have any family?" Lisa said rollin' over. She heard the whole conversation.

"Huh?"

"Why did you lie to me? You have a *brother*?" Lisa asked, lookin' deep into Bryan's eyes, showin' him the pain inside her from bein' deceived. "A brother? I don't want to live another lie. My ex-husband lied to me for years. Why did you have to lie to me about havin' a brother? If you'll lie to me about havin' a brother, you'll lie to me about anything. You can trust me, please don't hurt me. If we're going to be in this relationship, we have to be honest with each other."

"Lisa baby, look, I've had to lie about my uncle and my brother for years. My uncle killed a cop and my brother has been a well known Vice Lord since middle school. I'd never got a job in law enforcement if people knew. So I've just had to keep it a secret," he explained.

"And you don't feel like you could trust me?" she asked wit' tears beginnin' to well up in her eyes.

"It's not that. I ain't been able to keep it a secret for

years by tellin' every pretty lady I meet," Bryan said, touchin' her face, leanin' in, kissin' her on the cheek. "Okay? I'll never lie to you about nothin' else, cool?" he asked and she shook her head "yes".

"A'ight then baby. I'm 'bout to get in the shower," Bryan said, getting' up headed for the bathroom....

After Lisa heard the water in the shower runnin', she went through his cell phone to see what else he was lyin' about.

CHAPTER 41

FBI Headquartes, Chicago office.....

"....We're taking over and that's the end of it!" SAC Montgomery replied.

"We still have jurisdiction, one of my detectives was brutally murdered last night!" Chief Bridges shot back.

"This is a federal investigation," Montgomery responded.

"As of when?" Captain Jacobs asked, poundin' his fist on the table as his face turned red.

"As of now! Your guys have done nothing but fuck this whole investigation up! Someone in your little specialized unit has been swapping cocaine out the evidence room and leaking the identity of the informants, possibly even killing them. It's highly likely you have a murderer on your task force. Being that kilograms of cocaine is involved, it's a federal case. This investigation will not be compromised any further due to dirty cops under your command!" Agent Montgomery yelled.

"What the hell are you tryin' to say?" Jacobs asked, getting' in Montgomery's face.

"I think I've said it! Your task force is under investigation. All this bullshit has been going on under *your* watch," Montgomery responded, pointin' his finger dead in Jacob's chest.

"Settle down, settle down. We're all on the same team here. One of my detectives was killed last night. He had fucking kids man, 2 pretty little girls. *I* had to go knock on his wife's door. I just want the mother fucker who did it held responsible. However, it has to be done, let's do it," Chief Bridges said, steppin' in between the two tryin' to prevent them from comin' to blows.

"The only way it can be done is for us to take over. There's a leak in the task force and we have information that homicide is shaky too. I have an agent investigating now, and we have some informants in place. We're already making progress."

"And you'll be sharing all information with us, correct?" Captain Jacobs asked.

"Uuuuh, that will be a negative," Montgomery responded arrogantly.

"Goddamnitt Montgomery!" Jacobs exploded.

"Didn't I just tell you that there's leaks in your task force. I'm not taking any risk of our informants being murdered. I have one of my best agents on this. As soon as enough evidence is gathered, we'll make the arrest, and the list of charges will be long. I expect you to turn over all your files on your informants and on this Ryan Williams guy. You *will* share all your information with us. If you hold back one little crumb, I will bring you up on obstruction. Do I make myself clear captain?" Montgomery said, maintaining eye contact wit' Jacobs.

"Fuck you Montgomery," Jacobs said, storming out of the room. Chief Bridges just stood there for a second then he left shaking his head in disgust without saying another word.

CHAPTER 42

Nichole and R-Dubb's crib.....

"So what 'chu gonna be doin' today? Nichole asked, standin' in front of the dresser mirror puttin' her earrings in, getting ready for work.

"Thinking about you," Ryan responded, caressin' her from behind, kissin' her neck as she tilted her head to guide the earring through her piercing.

"Aw, you so sweet. I'm gonna be thinkin' about you too," she said, turnin' around wrappin' her arms around his neck plantin' tender kisses on his lips.

"Why you gotta go in all early-n-shit?" Ryan asked, really wantin' her to stay at home wit' him.

"I miss my babies, you pulled me away from 'em all weekend. I gotta check on 'em! Them ho's at work be done killed 'em. It's a shame. Them bitches don't really care 'bout them kids," Nichole explained. Those are her babies for real. She truly loves takin' care of those kids. They helped her get through them lonely days when Ryan was gone. She would just throw herself into her work, puttin' all her love and her time into the kids.

"Them kids gonna be a'ight," Ryan pouted as he grabbed a couple jars of X-pills.

"Boy quit trippin," Nikki responded as she headed for the kitchen, puttin' her salad and chicken pita's in her lunch bag. "I need to go to the grocery store," she said, takin' a look in the refrigerator.

"I'm headin' over to Merrillville. I'm gonna grind out of the hotel. I'll be up over there all day. Why don't I just take you to work? You can call me when you take your break and I'll come eat wit'cha."

"Sounds good to me," Nikki responded, grabbin' her lunch and her purse headin' for the door wit' Ryan right behind her.

"Let's take your car, I don't want draw all that attention to myself."

"Okay," Nichole responded as they walked out the do'. They hopped in the ride and headed for Merrillville Methodist Hospital and as Ryan was drivin' through Gary, his phone rang.....

"Damn nigga, you up off vacation yet?" Chi-Murder asked, not givin' Dubb a chance to say hello.

"Shit nigga, I miss you too," Dubb responded laughin' into the phone.

"Naw, ya'll have a nice time though?" Murder asked.

"Hell yeah, it was phat-n-a-bitch down there!"

"That's what's up, but dig. A nigga need you right now," Murder responded.

"It's all good too. I got whatever."

"Shiiiit, I need like 20 if you can stand it. Muh fuckaz is

tryin' to come up right now."

"I need 300," Dubb replied runnin' numbers through his head as he continued to drive his wife to work.

"That's what's up. Bout how long?"

"Gimmie an hour," Dubb replied.

"A'ight then, fa'sho folks."

"There you go wit' that bullshit," Ryan said laughin' as he hung up the phone. Him and Nichole rode for another 10 minutes or so then they pulled up at the hospital.

"Gimmie some suga Mommi!" Ryan said leanin' in givin' Nichole a deep tongue kiss.

"Mmmm," Nichole responded, rubbin' the back of his head as she kissed him back. "Bye Daddy. I'll call you when it's about lunch time. I'll have an hour," she said, getting' out the car.

"About what time? So I'll know not to be caught up in nothing," Dubb yelled out to her.

"At like 6 or 7. I love you," she yelled back to him, blowin' a kiss and wavin' goodbye.

"I love you too," Dubb responded, hollerin' back to her out the window as he pulled off drivin' back to Gary to get all the cocaine he needed for everybody. He hit Maniac and H.B. to see what they needed and he grabbed 2 bricks for J-Dogg and 1 for Nichole. He went on ahead and snatched up the last 50 pounds of weed too...

Everything went smooth, he sold Chi-Murder and Maniac 20 bricks a piece for $300,000. On top of that, Maniac needed another 40 pounds and 2 jars of X. Dubb slid it to him for $26,500. Dubb on top of the world right now. He ain't never made money like this. It just goes to show, wit' the right plug, a nigga can make it happen. A 'lil later on, Dubb dipped through the valley and J-Dogg had all his money plus some. So Dubb went ahead and told him the first package was a gift. J-Dogg paid him in full, $37,000 for two chickens and the last 10 pounds of weed. He on his feet now. After hookin' up wit' J-Dogg, Dubb shot back out to the telly to sell H.B. 10 ki's for $150,000. Shit's goin' good. Wit' the $250,000 he had when him and Nikki got back from the Circle City Classic, plus everything he made today, he got enough dough to slide Bryan a million dollars, buy Nichole's whip, and still have 28 thousand dollars and some change left. Plus he still sittin' on 147 bricks! That boy ballin!

CHAPTER 43

The Merrillville Inn.....

"What's goin' on bruh?" Bryan asked as Dubb answered the phone.

"Shit, just chillin'. Just got done countin' over a million nigga!"

"You bullshittin', what the fuck you be doin' wit' that shit?" Bryan asked in disbelief.

"My hustle hand is piss nigga," Dubb said kicked back feelin' himself a lil' bit right now. He made like $800,000 today. Who wouldn't be feelin' theyself?

"You got the money for that 'Maro?"

"Yep, I had the bread for that this morning," Dubb responded.

"Cool, the ride is at the crib, parked in the garage. Just leave the money for me, 35 exactly like I said.

"Hell yeah bruh, good lookin," Dubb said.

"That muh fucka ready too. It got the chip in it and everything. I ran the hell out that bitch on the highway.

"For real?"

"Hell yeah. Check it out when you go pick it up."

"That's what it do," Dubb responded.

"And check this out nigga. Switch phones. I got a bad vibe on something! I'm checkin' on some shit right now. I'll let you know what's hap'nin soon as I find out. But throw that bitch away, get you another one and leave the number wit' the bread. If what I think is up, you got til tomorrow before your shit is tapped. Throw that bitch away. You might even need to hit everybody you do bid'ness wit' from a payphone. Give them your new number, and tell 'em don't call you until they switch their shit out too. Handle that shit now, don't be bullshittin'."

"Shit, what's up?" Dubb asked wonderin' what the fuck is goin' on.

"Just do like I said bruh. I'll let you know. I gotta run and get back to work. I'll be in touch."

"A'ight bruh," Dubb said then hung up.

Immediately, he did just like his brother said. He drove strait to the Value-Mart 24 hour shoppin' center and bought 2 cell phones, one to keep in touch wit' Nichole and for regular everyday use and the other one for bid'ness. Then he got on the payphone and hit everybody up givin' them his new number and told them to switch up phones too. After that, he drove on over to the trap house to pick Nikki's ride up……

Gotdamn! This muh fucka is RAW! Dubb thought to hisself as he walked into the garage. Bryan's description didn't do the ride no justice. The paint looks like it got a couple extra clear coats on it. Glossy as Fuck…..

CHAPTER 44

FBI Headquarters, Chicago office.....

"What do you have for me?" SAC Montgomery asked as he answered his phone.

"Well, we need warrants to monitor Bryan's cell phone. Are you ready?" Agent Locke responded.

"Go ahead," Montgomery said, prepared to write the number down.

"(219) 555-6387 and his brother's phone number (219) 555-2954. Bryan is definitely stealing seized cocaine and is supplying his twin brother. I double checked. Jamal Byrd *was* arrested Saturday night and his shipment of 200 kilo's was intercepted by Bryan and his team. The question I have is why weren't we involved in the bust? 200 kilos, that is most definitely our jurisdiction."

"That whole task force is under investigation," Montgomery responded.

"Do we have enough manpower for surveillance?"

"Not at this time, no, but if we get something from the phones, we'll do surveillance and go after a search warrant if we can find out where the drugs are located. Good work! Report back as you gather more information."

"Thank you sir," Agent Locke said, hangin' up the phone.

CHAPTER 45

Lunch time.....

"Uhh, who is this?" Nichole answered her phone all defensive and shit, not recognizin' the number.

"It's me!" Dubb said.

"Who the fuck is me and how'd you get my number?" Nikki snapped.

"Girl, it's your husband. You ain't recognize my voice?"

"Aw boy! I didn't know this number. What happened to your phone? I'm on break. I been tryin' to call you."

"'B' called and told me I need to switch my shit up. This is my new number. Lock it in."

"Okay, how close are you? I'm out front talkin' to Theresa and 'nem!"

"I'm pullin' up now," Dubb said, smilin' anticipating' her reaction.

"Where? I don't see you," Nichole said, lookin' both ways in the street for her car.

"You looked right at me," Dubb said, stoppin' the Camaro right in front of her.

"Now that's my car right there! Daaamn baby, this *baaaad* ass car. I don't know what the fuck it is, it looks kinda like a charger or somethin'. Naw, it's one of them new Camaros. It just pulled up in front of me, man I wish it was my sh.....," she froze in shock as Dubbed rolled down the window, smilin' at her.

"Heeeeell naaaww!" Nikki said, hangin' up her phone. "When you get this?" She asked excited for her man.

"It's yours," Dubb said, gettin' out the car holdin' the door open for her.

"Aaaah," she gasped, holdin' her hands in front of her mouth. "For real baby, this is mine?"

"All yours baby, get in, take me for a ride," Dubb said walkin' around getting' in the passenger side of the car. "Go 'head Mommi, get in. It's all yours," Ryan said as Nichole got in the driver's seat feelin' like a boss bitch, experiencin' the power of the engine as it grumbled from the loud flow master pipes. Baby girl dropped the car in gear and peeled off the lot.

"Aaaaaaay!" Nichole screamed as she drove the Camaro up the street.

"Your sounds is pumpin' too, turn 'em on," Dubb laughed as Nichole pushed the power button on the C.D. player. "Addicted to Money" by Lil' Scrappy featuring Ludacris came bangin' from the trunk shakin' the whole ride. She got 3 12 inch kicker competition subwoofers in the trunk powered by their new 2,500 watt competition amp. She got mid's and high's with a digital crossover and the power to push 'em. Baby girl's shit sounds nice. Everything's loud and crystal clear.

"Fuck this shit, I ain't goin' back to work tonite," Nikki said, turnin' the music down, callin' the hospital on her cell phone....

"Methodist Hospital, Shirley speaking," the director of nurses answered.

"Hey gurl, this is Nichole. I need to take a half of a vacation day. Matter-of-fact, a day and a half. I ain't comin' to work tomorrow either."

"Is somethin' wrong honey? You *never* miss," Shirley said.

"Oh no, everything is *fine*. My man is home! I been savin' up my vacation time just for this.

"You go girl. I'll cover your shifts, and we'll see you, um, Wednesday?" Shirley responded.

"Yep."

"Alright, have a nice time honey. Bye, bye."

"Thanks," Nichole said as she hung up.

"Thank you Daddy," Nichole said, givin' Ryan a kiss while they were stopped at the light, still hardly able to grasp the fact that the car is hers.

"So, what we finna do?" Dubb asked her.

"We finna ride baby! I need to stop by the house and change. Do I got anything left? I sold the last five ounces I had at work," Nichole said as she gripped the steering wheel.

"Yep, I grabbed another brick for you today," Dubb

responded.

"Cool, I need to stop by Alexis' crib to get my money and give her some more."

"That's what's up," Dubb said as Nichole guided the machine up the street. "Oh yeah, we need to stop by Bryan's spot to pick up the Aurora.

"Okay," Nichole said, turnin' the music back up, mashin' the gas, lettin' the pipes growl as she ripped up the street.

CHAPTER 46

Bob's Burger Joint.....

"So what's the deal?" Bryan asked Tim as he took a big bite of his burger while they sat inside Bryan's favorite greasy burger joint. Timothy Cohen is a computer wizard. He's a member of the computer crimes unit. He tracks down sick muh fuckaz who download child porn and muh fuckaz who use computers to commit white collar crimes. He's an expert hacker and believe me, he gets his! He knows how to run some high-tech shit called "worms". Nobody knows but Bryan. They were investigatin' a high level drug dealer who was movin' money by electronic transfer all over the world. Right before they popped his ass off, Cohen intercepted one of his transfers. He kicked Bryan out a couple hundred G's, and they been cool ev'ry since.

"You're not going to like this," Cohen said, sippin' his Starbucks latte' and lookin' frazzled as usual. He was tryin' to organize his file.

"What is it?" Bryan asked, chompin' his burger and growin' impatient.

"That little girlfriend of yours is not who she says she is," Cohen said, throwin' a picture of a white, blonde chick with blue eyes on the table. "Unless she came all the way to the windy city to get a tan," Cohen said sarcastically.

"What the fuck?" Bryan said in disbelief. "Who the fuck is this?"

"That's the real Lisa Kelley. When I first started checkin'

her out, your girlfriend's picture showed up. Nice, pretty black chick. It's too easy. My 9 year old can manipulate the internet so *my* picture shows up when somebody Googles *you*. So, I dug deeper. They expected you to check her out with the Maryland Bar. That's why they used a real person's identity. When I hacked into the bar association's database, I got that picture."

"Ain't that a bitch?" Bryan said, shakin' his head.

"Oh, there's more," Timothy said, pausing as he fumbled through his stack of papers. "Once I saw that picture, all kinds of red flags popped up. So, I ran the cell number you gave me, and I got nothing, zilch, zero. There were no incoming calls except yours, and she calls nobody but you. That made me really suspicious. I was able to use the home phone and her e-mail address to hack into her computer system. Here's what I found," Cohen said, slidin' the file across the table. "Her real name is Amber Locke. She's been a federal agent for 7 years. I got me a couple new toys. I sat outside her house and listened to her phone conversations and I overheard this," Cohen said, pushin' play on the mini-recorder.....

"Well, we need warrants to monitor Bryan's cell phone, are you ready?" he heard his girlfriend's voice.

"Go ahead," went a man's voice.

"(219) 555-6387 and his brother's phone number, (219) 555-2954. Bryan is definitely stealing seized cocaine and is supplying his twin brother...."

"Fuck!" Bryan said, poundin' his fist on the table after listenin' to Agent Locke's conversation. "That bitch gotta go."

"Thanks man, you the coldest to ever do this shit," Bryan

said.

"Don't thank me, pay me," Cohen said. wit' his hand out. He was waitin' on Bryan to give him an envelope wit' 50, one-hundred dollar bills in it.....

CHAPTER 47

Ouside Alexis' 'nem house.....

"Hell naw, Nichole look!" Dubb said, crackin' up and pointin' at Alexis' house as they were pullin' up. "It look like Ayzia and her husband Shaheim out on the porch Fightin'. She whuppin' his ass too. DAAAMNN!" Dubb said, laughin' even harder as Ayzia stole dude dead in the mouth. "I mean, the bitch tagged him and squared off in front of him wit' her hands up. Hell naw!" Dubb said, continuin' to laugh while slappin' his knee.

"What the fuck's goin' on?" Nichole asked, gettin' out the car.

"Fuck this ugly black ass nigga! He getting the fuck up outta here. Stayin' out all night. I told the bitch to have his ass home when I called," Ayzia said, goin' back in the house and grabbin' some trash bags filled with clothes. She came back outside and threw 'em on the porch.

"So what I ain't come home last night. You be fuckin' niggaz all up in the strip club-n-shit," Shaheim said, tryin' to defend himself.

"Bitch! Ain't nobody doin' no fuckin' up in this muh fucka but *me*. You the bitch of this relationship. You knew I sold pussy when you married me!" Ayzia said, kickin' his clothes around on the porch and scatterin' them around as they fell out the bags. "I pay the cost to be the boss 'round this bitch! I'll fuck when I get ready. You can't do what I do. And, when I see that ho, I'm fuckin' her up! You *my* husband.....matter-of-fact."

"Aw hell naw," Dubb said crackin' up. He was laughin' so hard he almost fell out the car as Ayzia ran up on dude and grabbed him by the ear like he's a lil' kid-n-shit.

"Get your lil' bitch ass in the house. We finna call that ho and you gonna tell her.....,"
Ayzia snapped, draggin' Shaheim in the house by his ear.

"Hold on baby, I'll be back," Nikki told Dubb through a laugh while she went towards the house to handle her bid'ness.

Dubb just sat in the car laughin' to himself while he waited. *Ain't no way I'd marry that ho. That boy KNEW she be sellin' pussy and he be layin' up wit' her, tongue kissin' her, eew. And homegirl be braggin' 'bout how he be eatin' her out. Ain't no way in hell......*

He sat in the car thinkin' to himself and listenin' to music while he waited on Nikki to come back to the car.......

"Aw hell naw, you bitch!" Alexis yelled at Nichole as she came outside to see the ride. This muh fucka is clean bitch! Look at ya'll. Ya'll niggaz is doin' too much!" Alexis said, shakin' her head, trippin' off the car.

"Don't hate baby, don't hate," Nichole said, jokin' wit' her.

"Gurl, you shittin' on these bitches right now. Niggaz too. This ride is nasty," Alexis said lookin' it over.

"Tell Ryan what you told me," Nichole said to Alexis.

"Hey Dubb, you know this Mexican named Chico? He from Cosecho, Coshiedo Park or however the fuck you say it?"

Alexis said, leanin' in the passenger side of the car.

"Yeah, he Latin Lings from East Chicago. He be movin' weight," Dubb responded.

"Yeppurr! That's him. The muh fucka hatin' on you. He be trickin' wit' me and I heard him talkin'. He put $50,000 on your head. He said you doin' too much and puttin' a dent in his pockets," Alexis explained as Dubb listened wit' his face frowned up.

"Aw yeah?" Dubb responded as he immediately began to plot on dude.

"Fa'sho. You my nigga. Nikki like my sister. I'm tellin' you 'cause you like family nigga," Alexis said.

"Good lookin'. Make sure you get a hold of me you hear somethin' else," Dubb responded.

"A'ight bitch. Get off my ride, you puttin' smudges on my shit," Nikki said, droppin' the ride in gear.

"Aw, my bad homie," Alexis said, breathin' on the door where she was leanin' and polishin' it wit' her shirt sleeve. "Bye bitch," she said, laughin'.

"Bye ho," Nichole said, pullin' off and lettin' the pipes holler.

"So where we goin' baby?" Dubb asked firin'up a Swisher.

"I don't know. I figure we'd drive to Chicago and grab somethin' to eat. We can get a room and come back tomorrow……

CHAPTER 48

Wesley's Bar and Grill.....

"Damn baby, what took you so long to get here?" Bryan asked Lisa, Amber, or whoever the fuck the bitch really is as she reached the table. Tonite they have a date at Wesley's Bar and Grill. It's a blue room. It's where police officers go for food and drinks after work. He's respected as a good cop by most of the people inside the crowded establishment. The rest he hasn't had the opportunity to work with. Tonite is the nite! It's Monday nite football and the Bears is playin' the Colts.....

"I had a hard time figuring out what to wear," she said as Bryan helped her wit' her coat.

"I done drunk up all the beer already," Bryan said pourin' her the last glass and motionin' for the waitress to bring another pitcher.

"Has it started yet?" she asked, gettin' comfortable in their booth.

"Naw, not yet. But while we're waitin', umm, I been thinkin' about us a lot lately and I need to talk to you," Bryan said, touchin' her hand as he looked in her eyes.

"Well, talk to me. What's on your mind sweetie?" she responded.

"All that talk of wantin' to be in a commitment, and not wantin' to be on the datin' scene. How much of that is real?" Bryan asked while holdin' her hand.

"All of it. Why you ask?" she questioned, wonderin' where all this is goin'.

"Do you believe that some people are just made for each other and life is just too short to play games? And, when two people are given the opportunity for love, they should take it?"

"Yes," she responded, smiling as they continued to hold hands.

"Do you believe we have the opportunity for love?"

"Yes," she said, thinkin' to herself how much of a sucker for love Bryan is and how she's gonna get all the information she needs to bring him and his brother down.

"I know this is a little soon, but life is short," Bryan said, steppin' out the booth, gettin' down on one knee and openin' up a jewelry box wit' a nice 2 carat engagement ring. "Lisa, will you marry me?" Bryan asked as damn near everybody in the bar looked on....

"Say yes honey!" some wife of a retired cop cheered, chompin' on her gum all decked out in Chicago Bears gear.

"What 'chu waitin' on baby doll. Say yes before I do," yelled another old lady.

"For cryin' out loud, say yes for Christ sakes. The game's about to start," Captain Jacobs said as everyone in the bar started laughin'.

"Will you marry me?" Bryan asked again, pushin' the box towards her.

"Bryan are you drunk?" she asked, smilin' at him.

"Yeah," he answered, as the crowd gathered around and began laughin' again.

"Yes! Yes, I'll marry you!" the stankin' ass bitch answered, acceptin' the ring while huggin' and kissin' him like she's really in love. The whole place cheered and everyone celebrated by sendin' the newly engaged couple shots.

They drank and watched the game while they ate basket after basket of wings and fries. The Bears lost 13 to 7 and the crowd was pissed.....

"Bryan honey, it's getting' late and I have to be up early tomorrow for a couple interviews. I better get home," she said, kissin' him and feelin' a lil' sick. She figures she ate too many wings and drank too much beer.

"Are you okay to drive," Bryan asked wit' concern on his voice.

"Yeah, I'm fine."

"Call me. Let me know you made it home safe. I'll be over later.

"Okay," she said, peckin' him on the lips again.

Bryan stayed at the bar all night, getting' sloppy drunk and celebratin' wit' the fellas. He's so drunk that Sergeant Ortiz wouldn't let him drive to Lisa's house. He offered to give him a ride.....

CHAPTER 49

Chi-Town.....

Nikki was feelin' good-n-a-bitch. She was flyin' high as she pulled onto the streets of Chicago. She knows her ride's the shit. Heads are turnin' as her 24 inch Diablo's cut the light shinnin' down on them from the street lamps. Her and Dubb bent corners blowin' on Swisha Sweets as they gazed at the store fronts. Nicole finally decided to stop at a nice, cozy diner and a movie spot. It's a classy 'lil restaurant where you kick off your shoes and literally hop in the bed and watch a movie on the large theatre sized screen while you eat. Currently, the restaurant is showin' that new movie starin' Mo'nique called "Precious". Its about a young, black, overweight teenage mother wit' low self-esteem. It's expected to win several awards. The film's been getting' rave reviews from the critics.

After they got settled in, Ryan ordered a 14 oz t-bone steak wit' a side of king crab legs, and Nichole ordered grilled chicken and shrimp. They laid there on the king sized bed feeding each other and watchin' the movie.

CHAPTER 50

Lisa's house.....

"I'm really happy for you Wilkins. I mean, Lisa is a *beautiful* woman," Sergeant Ortiz of the Chicago Vice Squad said while he was pullin' up in front of Lisa's house.

"Yeah, I know it. She's b-e-ua-t-ful," Bryan slurred, leanin' his head against the passenger side window. "I got llu-cky maaan sheeeez hot."

"Damn, you're trashed bro. Let me get you to the door," Ortiz grunted as he got out the car.

"Na-naww maan, I'm okay. I'm really okay," Bryan continued to slur his words as the sergeant helped him out of the car.

"The hell you are, c'mon," Ortiz said, guidin' him to the door.

"Heeeey maaan, w-we, we gonna have a helll-uvvv-a, batch-lor par-ty," Bryan said staggering as they reached the porch.

"You got a key?" Ortiz asked.

"Ummm, nope," Bryan said, off balance bracin' himself against the sergeant.

"Okay, I guess we'll just have to ring the door be....," Ortiz stopped mid-sentence, seein' the front door is cracked open with the frame split. Evidently it was split from being kicked in. "Stay here Wilkins. Stay here!" Ortiz instructed as he entered the house with his weapon drawn.

"Lisa!" he called out as he crouched through the living room.

"Liiissaaaa!" he shouted again, bracin' himself against a wall before turning the corner, pointin' his gun as he noticed the staircase to his right.

"Liiiissssaaaa!" he called out again as he made his way up the stairs, staying close to the wall and holding his pistol close to his face like the cops do on T.V.

He reached the top of the stairs and started pokin' in and out of the doorways. Then he reached the 4th door which was cracked open a few inches. He gently pushed the door open and eased into the room.....

Shit! He cursed to himself. The room had been trashed. Lamps were knocked over, and the covers were ripped off the bed. Sergeant Ortiz immediately ran downstairs to Bryan and they rushed to the car to call it in.....

This is sergeant Ortiz, number 8124, Chicago Vice. I'm reporting a possible abduction, 3692 Oakwood Lane. I want the crime lab out here *now*. We have an officer's fiancée involved," Ortiz barked over the radio.

"Yes sir sergeant. Units are on the way, the dispatcher responded.

"It's gonna be okay buddy. It's gonna be okay," Ortiz consoled Bryan as he was humped over, throwin' up in the street.

"Naw man, I'm goin' in there. Liiisa!!" Bryan called out as he attempted to get past Ortiz.

"Calm down man. There might be evidence in there that can help us find her. You're gonna mess up the crime scene. Just pipe down and mellow out!" Ortiz yelled at Bryan, holdin' him back.

"Liiiiiiisssaaa!" Bryan cried out at the top of his lungs.

"Look at me!" Ortiz said, holdin' Bryan by the shoulders and shakin' some sense into him. "We're going to find her. Just try to relax man. Just try to relax.

"She's gonna be my wife man. What the fuck!" Bryan said, falling to the ground and pounding his fist on the pavement.

"Crime lab's gonna be here in a second bro, just be cool alright? Here man, have a seat in the car," Ortiz said, helping Bryan up and opening the car door.......

CHAPTER 51

Meanwhile…

After the movie, Ryan and Nicole relaxed in their suite at the Radisson Inn. They were talkin' and sippin' on some bubbles as they sat in the hot tub…..

"….that movie was kinda sad though. I felt sorry for Precious," Nichole said.

"Yeah, Mo'nique was hell wasn't she?"

"That's my bitch though. That heifer crazy," Nichole responded.

"Naw, your girl *Ayzia* crazy," R-Dubb said as Nikki damn near spit her drink into their bath water from laughin'.

"Naw, naw, look," Nikki said, crackin' up. "I told you how she posts all her business up on Twitter right?"

"Yeah, I remember you tellin' me about that shit," Dubb replied.

"A'ight look--this bitch," Nicole said, takin' a sip from her glass. "This bitch done went online postin' messages. 'Bitch it's on and I'm ridin' tonight,' and 'You might have had him once but I got him all the time'," Nichole said, laughin'.

"Hell naw, what's wrong wit' her?" Dubb asked.

"The bitch crazy. I hope Tiffany put her car up tonite cause Ayzia talkin' 'bout flattenin' that bitch tires and pourin' sugar in her tank. Ayzia a drama queen. It's on for real. Every time she see Tiffany, it's gonna be some shit."

"But hold up though. I don't understand it. Don't that bitch be fuckin' niggaz and sellin' pussy up in the strip club?" Dubb asked.

"Shoot, I don't understand either. I guess she feels like she's the nigga in that relationship. Shaheim's *her* bitch. She's what? 35, and he's like 23, 24 years old? Yeah, she said *she's* runnin' that shit," Nichole explained.

"That's crazy," Dubb responded as he gulped the last of his Don Peringon and reached for the bottle.

"She feel like she pays the bills. I mean dude *really-is-her-lil'-bitch*! He don't pay for shit, don't buy no food, nothin'. She buys that niggaz clothes. She buys his video games, his weed, his lil' jewelry, and she just bought him a new scooter this past summer, not no cheap one either," Nichole said countin' on her fingers as she broke it down. "She takes care of *her* bitch," Nikki said wit' a lil' laugh.

"Hell naw, you say that shit like you think it's cool. They married."

"I don't think it's cool. I think it's funny. That's them. That's what works for them. I literally log onto Twitter everyday to see what that bitch goin' through. And I ain't bullshittin', thousands you hear me? That bitch gets thousands of views everyday. Muh fuckaz from all over the world be tweetin', sendin DM's and respondin' to her drama," Nichole explained.

"For real?" Dubb asked in disbelief.

"Yep. She'll be like, 'I got a call, my hubby is over this bitch named Rochelle's house. I'm going to go get him and beat her ass! And muh fuckaz be responding to that shit. They be sayin' 'beat her ass', and 'you go girl." I be trippin' out over that shit. Ayzia like a internet star."

"Hell naw," Dubb said, dryin' his hands off and firin' up a Swisher. "That's a weak nigga though. Ain't no muh fuckin' way I'd marry no stripper wit' 8,9,10 kids and 12 baby daddies who be sellin' pussy. Pimp her yeah, marry her no, hell naw!" Dubb said, inhalin' the smoke.

"Shit, he a lil' boy. Won't no nigga her age fuck wit' her so she snatched up a lil' youngsta she can *try* to control. Armani put her up on that shit," Nikki said as Ryan gave her the Swisha. "Ew, ew, I almost forgot. Ayzia drug that nigga to the computer and sat him down in front of the webcam and made him do a video blog proclaimin' his love for Ayzia and how he don't ever wanna see Tiffany no more."

"Hell naw."

"I told you. While you was gone, some days I'd just get me a drink and go over there and sit. It's better than T.V. That shit you saw today goes down all the time."

"That shit *was* funny though," Dubb said as Nichole passed the Swisha back.

"Alexis trippin', actin' all 'noid and shit over what happened to ole girl's snitchin' ass. You know they was fuckin'."

"Whaaat?" Dubb responded in disbelief.

"Yeah, Alexis called herself likin' the bitch," Nichole said, getting' out the tub. "She said she's done wit' bitches though," Nichole said, walkin' out the bathroom.

"Hold on baby, where you goin'?" Dubb said while his eyes followed his wife's booty as it jiggled into the bedroom.

"I'm goin' to bed and I ain't sleepy neither," Nichole said as she peeked around the corner smilin' at him, motionin' for him to 'come here' wit' her finger.

CHAPTER 52

Where's Lisa.....

The crime lab showed up in a matter of minutes as well as various detectives and uniformed cops, all showing support for their colleague. The crime lab processed the scene thoroughly, takin' special care because this investigation involves the fiancée of one of their own. Sadly, there's not much to go on. Neighbors stated they seen a mysterious black man close the lid of his trunk and drive off in a dark colored late model sedan around 12:45 a.m. Crime lab detectives didn't find any blood or semen in the bedroom. There were fingerprints all over the place, but more than likely, they belonged to Lisa. Bryan gave a tape-recorded statement of tonight's events, which was corroborated by various officers who appeared at the scene. Everyone expressed their condolences. This is truly a tragic incident. The couple was just engaged hours earlier. It was picture perfect. They looked so happy together as they celebrated their engagement amongst members of Chicago's finest. The wedding was sure to be nothing short of spectacular, attended by hundreds of police throughout the Chicago and northwestern Indiana area. Detective Sergeant Brian Wilkins has gained a lot of respect due to his outstanding detective work in the area over the years. After the investigation for the night came to a close, Sergeant Ortiz gave Bryan a ride home, counseling him and assuring him that the perpetrator of this heinous crime would be brought to justice. "One way or another," Sergant Ortiz said givin' Bryan "the look". At times like this, the cops will hold court on the streets murdering the suspect in cold blood and plantin' a gun in his hand. The sergeant walked his fellow officer to the door huggin' him and shakin' his hand. He swore on his badge that he would get to the bottom of this. Then he turned to leave.....

Dummies, the whole thing played out perfect! Bryan thought to himself as he undressed for bed. See, after he met wit' Timothy Cohen, he went to see "Merk". That's what he does, merk people. He'll kill anybody for the right price. He was lucky tonite. He didn't even have to kill nobody. Bryan gave him sixty-five thousand dollars, just to make Lisa disappear.

When Bryan saw Lisa, well Agent Locke, enter the bar, he saw that as the perfect opportunity to slip that *shit* in the last lil' bit of beer he was drinkin' on, and he poured her a glass. It's some kind of slow actin' poison. It's tasteless and it takes a few hours to take effect. It's highly toxic and it's easily detected in the blood stream. That's why it's so important her body is *never* found and no blood was at the scene. The job was easy. Amber was dead damn near before her head touched the pillow. All Merk had to do was make it look like there was a struggle and carry Amber's lifeless body outside, dump her in the trunk and dispose of the body where it will never, ever, *ever* be found.

How I played that engagement shit? Aw man, I'm colder than Denzel! Playin' the happily, newly engaged couple role in front of all of them sworn officers of the law? How I stayed at the bar getting' drunk and havin' a vice squad detective take me to Amber's house to make the "shocking discovery?" That part wasn't planned, but it sure worked out good. Oh yeah, I'm cold. Bryan laughed to himself as he drifted off to sleep.

CHAPTER 53

Tuesday Morning, FBI Headquarters, Chicago.....

"Goddamnitt! I want some fucking answers! One of my agents, one of my *best* agents, came up missing in the middle of the night?" SAC Montgomery yelled as his blubbery face turned beat red.

"How the fuck was we supposed to know she was your agent? If you would've shared your sensitive little information with us, we could've put some protection on her," Chief Bridges responded.

"Yeah right. I've seen your *protection*. The last time the Snitch Killer struck, he killed your *protection*," Montgomery shot back staring Bridges down.

"Fuck you Montgomery! That's why we hate working with you fucking, fucking, federal agents. You always blame your shit on us. How in the *hell* is it our screw up that your agent is missing and we didn't even know she was an agent?" Captain Jacobs responded. "We didn't know who she was, *period*!"

"I bet your prized Detective Sergeant Wilkins knows what happened to her," Montgomery spat.

"What the fuck kind of unfounded implication is that? Sergeant Wilkins was with us at Wesley's Bar and Grill all night. He just proposed to your agent. He was in love with her! He celebrated with a bar full of officers all night and Sergeant Ortiz took him to your agent's house and that's when they discovered her home had been broken into. Evidently, your agent was using inappropriate methods during her investigation. There's no tellin' who all she's slept with that could've wanted to harm her."

"What's that supposed to mean?" Montgomery asked defensively.

"For Christ sakes, she was fuckin' her subject. Her and Wilkins were sleeping together. What, you thought he fell in love with her smile," Jacobs responded throwin' his hands in the air.

"You watch your fucking mouth!" Montgomery said, moving towards Jacobs. "Agent Locke is a very professional agent and there's no way in hell she'd sleep with a low-life scumbag like Bryan Wilkins. You just need to make sure *your* officers are who they say they are!"

"What are you saying?" Chief Bridges asked, confused as to what the agent is trying to say.

"At this point, I'm not saying a word. I will not let you cluster fucks fuck up my investigation any further. One of my agents is missing if not dead, and I'm going to solve this case."

"One of my detectives *is* dead," Bridges responded. "We want it solved just as bad as you do."

"Oh no you don't. You're not going to like the light my investigation is going to shine on your homicide and task force units."

"What the fuck is that supposed to mean?"

"You'll see. But for now, both of you jack offs can get the

hell out of my office," Montgomery ordered as he pointed at the door.

"This is a crock of shit," Jacobs mumbled under his breath as him and Chief Bridges stormed through the door.

CHAPTER 54

Back in Chi-Town.....

"C'mon girl. You better hurry your ass up," Dubb called to the bathroom as he rolled up a couple Swisha's for their hour long trip back to Gary. *That girl always take fo'ever.*

"So what we doin' today?" Nichole yelled to him from the bathroom as she finished up her hair.

"I don't know. Whatever you wanna do. I don't have no plans or nowhere to be," Ryan said as Nichole came out the bathroom.

"Why don't we just go back home, go to the grocery store, and cook up somethin' to eat on all day. Then we can go to the video store and rent some movies," she said as she sat on his lap. "I just wanna be all alone with you. I missed you so much," she said as she kissed him on the lips, touchin' his face.

"That's what's up. I'm down to spend the whole day wit' my honey bunny."

"You promise? No phones, no runs, no nothin'. Just me and you all day?" Nichole asked.

"I promise. Just me and you."

"Aw yeah, I been havin' a taste for some of that Chicago style pizza. Let's grab some before we leave," Nichole suggested.

"Shit, let's go before the cleanin' lady kick the do' in. We was supposed to *been* gone," Dubb said as they got up to leave. They left the hotel and found a nice lil' pizzeria on the east side of Chicago. They had pizza and beer. After their lil' lunch, they got on the highway and headed home....

"Thank you baby. I really *love* this car!" Nikki exclaimed as she pressed her foot on the gas.

"You welcome Mommi," Dubb said, laughin' as he silently prayed she didn't kill them on the way home.

CHAPTER 55

Task Force Headquarters.....

"Uhh, have a seat Wilkins," Jacobs sighed as he motioned to the chair across from his desk.

"After what happened last night, I suggest you take some time off. I know you were crazy about that woman.....

"Now hold up captain," Bryan interrupted.

"Wait 'til I'm finished, alright?" Captain Jacobs said. "I know this is a difficult time for you and you're not going to be able to focus on your investigations and you'll be distracted. I don't want your emotions getting in the way of this case," Captain Jacobs explained gently.

"Don't bullshit me captain. You don't give a *fuck* about emotions. Normally, you'd tell me to shake it off and get to work. Give it to me strait," Bryan responded.

"If you don't take off on sick leave claiming emotional distress until this shit storm passes over, I'll be forced to place you on unpaid suspension indefinitely," Jacobs shot it to him strait.

"What the fuck is this all about?" Bryan asked getting nervous as fuck, wonderin' what all the captain knows.

"I don't know what the fuck you've been up to, but I went to bat for your ass. I've gotten my ass chewed by the special agent in charge *twice*! Over allegations that there's some dirty cops on our task force and this morning, Agent

Montgomery implicated you specifically."

"What do you mean *agent*? Am I under some sort of investigation?" Wilkins asked, playin' dumb as fuck.

"This might be a hard pill for you to swallow, but Lisa is an F.B.I. Agent. Her name is Amber Locke and you were the target of her investigation. The Feds believe you had something to do with her disappearance. Chief Bridges and I stood up for you. Hell, you were with us all night. They also suspect you've been stealing narcotics and puttin' 'em back on the streets. They're speculating that you've either leaked the identities of the murdered informants or you've killed them yourself."

"What? Hold on. First of all, Lisa loves me. She is *not* an F.B.I. Agent! She's a recently divorced lawyer from Baltimore, and we *are* getting married. I-I just can't even believe you'd entertain any of that other bullshit," Bryan said as he stood up.

"I don't know my ass from a hole in the wall right now. All I know is that the pressure is on *me* right now. *My* ass is in the fuckin' sling! I gotta meet with mayor this morning. I think it's best you get the fuck out of the way until this shit blows over. Sweet Mary Mother of God, I hope you're clean. If not, you better hope the Feds get you before I do. I'm giving you the benefit of the doubt. The rest of the unit is getting transferred to various precincts to report for uniformed duty. I have no choice. Now get the fuck out of my office and get down to human resources and tell them uppity, pencil pushing bitches you're depressed and you're losing your fucking mind. Here's my letter of recommendation," Jacobs said, throwing the letter on his desk. He was looking down and fumbling through a stack of papers like Bryan ain't even there no more, lettin' him know the discussion is over.

CHAPTER 56

Quality time.....

Nikki and Dubb spent the whole day stuck up each other's ass.

When they got back to the 'G', they went strait to the video store and rented about 5 or 6 movies. Nichole wanted him to see some of the movies he missed out on while he was locked up. When Dubb was at "The City", they showed new releases on the institutional channels, but they didn't show every movie that came out then.

They strolled through the grocery store like the happy newlywed couple they are. They bought a large family pack of chicken wings to fry for the day and some other shit just to have some food in the house. Since Dubb was gone, there wasn't no reason for Nichole to do much cookin', so she wasn't stocked up on groceries.

After they left the grocery store, they stopped by the sex shop. Dubb insisted Nicole get a sexy lil' outfit to wear around the house tonite. So, she picked out some slutty porno star type shit wit' some high heels to match, and she grabbed Dubb a pair of matching silk boxers. They got some sex toys and some pornos so they could be nasty as fuck later on. They really enjoyed spendin' the whole day together. They got fucked up all day drinkin' and smokin' weed. On top of all the weed smoke and liquor, Dubb done popped one of them SpongeBob's and he rollin' like a muh fucka! They are fucked-the fuck-up! Nikki and Dubb laid on the couch cuddlin' and watchin' movies for awhile. Then, they sat up talkin', drinkin' Remy Martin V.S.O.P. and listenin' to music. They laughed and giggled like two teenagers in love. They talked about how much they loved each other. They swore to stay together forever and always remain faithful. The happy couple even talked about havin' kids sometime soon, and they even tried to figure out where they gonna move when they get their money together. After they finished cuddling and talking, they decided to take a shower and get dressed into their lil' outfits. Dubb loves the fact that Nikki knows how to mix it up. She read all kinds of sex and relationship books while Dubb was locked up, and she learned that every man wants a nasty lil' whore every now and then. She knows that if a man comes home to a good girl night after night, he's gonna find him a nasty lil' whore out in the streets. And as she puts on her bright red "hooker" lipstick, she feels like a nasty lil' whore in her red porn star outfit wit' her red fishnet thigh high stockings and 5 inch stilettos. Her pussy got hot and moist as she thought about all the nasty shit she's gonna do with her husband tonite.....

"Gotdamn!" Dubb said when Nikki walked into the livin' room in her outfit as his dick snapped to attention. She looks completely different, her hair, her makeup and everything.

"You like it?" Nichole asked, turnin' around, bendin' over a lil' bit and stickin' her ass out exposin' her booty cheeks and freshly waxed pussy lips. She ain't got no panties on. All she has on is the red lace corset, the stilettos and fish net stockings with the lil' clips holdin' 'em to her corset. Then, she turned and straddled Dubb, nibblin' on his neck......

"I'm not your wife tonight," she whispered in his ear. "I'm your nasty lil' bitch, your lil' whore. My name's Cherry," she said seductively, makin' Goosebumps break out all over his body. Then she kissed him thirstfully, trying to quench her desires by sucking Dubbs' tongue as she looked him in the eyes.

Shit! Was all Dubb could think to himself. "Cherry" got up and went over to the stereo and put on some "fuck music." It was a mix tape wit' shit on it like, "It feels so good," "Get It Wet," "Get it Wetter," by Twista, "Lollipop" by Lil' Wayne and "Bust It Baby" 1 and 2 by Plies, freaky shit to fuck to. She sauntered sexily to the DVD player, turnin' the pornos on the large plasma screen then she sat next to Dubb on the couch as bitches started gettin' the shit fucked out of them on the T.V. screen. She cocked her legs open, partin' her wet pussy lips. She took one of the blunts Dubb had rolled up on the coffee table and rubbed it all over her slit, getting' it soaked wit' her sweet, slimy pussy juice. Then, she dried it wit' a lighter as the aroma of her sweet pussy filled the air. She lit the tip of it, inhaling deeply. She exhaled the smoke through her nose and passed the Swisha to Dubb so he could get high off the weed laced with her intoxicating juices.

"Damn Mommi, I can taste your pussy," he said, puffin' on the cigarello. *DAMN she turnin' me on.*

"Is it good daddy?" she asked as her leg was still cocked up on the couch with her fingers gently rubbin' her clit. Not tryin' to cum, just teasin' herself as Dubb looked at her wit' a bulge in his draws. He was makin' a wet spot in his boxers from leakin' pre-cum out the tip of his dick. They sat there listenin' to the music, drinkin' and smokin' on the Swisher while watchin' the porno for like 20 minutes or so. Then "Cherry" decided to put on her own lil' show. She took the coffee table and turned it so it was facin' Dubb long ways. Then, she disappeared into the bedroom and returned with the bag of toys from the sex shop. She removed the vibrating double action dildo from the sack and put the batteries in it.

"Oh shit baby, you makin' me horny as fuck," Dubb said, hardly able to control himself. He wants to bang her pussy up on the coffee table right *now*!

"Unn uhn, not yet. Help me get the other part in my asshole," she instructed. She cocked her legs strait up in the air as Dubb got the sex lube out the bag. He was lickin' her asshole, rubbin' lil' circles around it, and lubricatin' her wit' the strawberry flavored lube. Then, he placed the tip of the smaller dildo in her asshole as the fat one slid in her drippy, wet pussy hole.

"Ooooh," Cherry moaned as she eased the vibrator inside both her fuck holes.

"Oooooooh, sssssssss," she hissed as she took the full length and started movin' it in and out while Dubb watched in a daze of sexual arousal as Cherry fucked herself. She was lovin' the feelin' of her pussy and her ass bein' filled at the same time. The vibrator got wetter and wetter wit' every stroke, as her whole slit became nice and slick from her pussy juice runnin' down her crack. It was mixin' wit' the sex lube as the vibrator moved in and out of both her openings.

"Damn baby," Dubb said.

"Unn uhn, call me Cherry. Call me a bitch," Nichole gasped as she stroked herself, becomin' lost in the role she's playin'.

"Damn bitch!"

"Oh yeah, oh yeah, oh *hell* yeah! Take your draws off. I-I wanna see you stroke your dick," she said, continuing to fuck both her holes as Dubb dropped his draws, strokin' the tip of his dick. His shit so hard it feels like it's finna break off!

"Eeeew stroke it nigga. I'm 'bout to cuuummmm,

sssssssshit!" she said, fuckin' herself as fast and hard as she could as she squirted pussy cum all over Dubb's legs while he stood directly in front of her.

"Damn bitch, you squirted across the room like the porno bitches do," Dubb said, droppin' to his knees, lickin' her juices, and stickin' his tongue deep inside her booty hole. It's still gaped open from bein' rammed wit' the dildo.

"Eew, let me taste *your* ass," Cherry said as she got up. "Turn around on the couch."

"Huh?" Dubb questioned.

"Turn around," she ordered, smackin' him on the ass. She guided him to the couch and leaned him over the back as his knees was on the cushions. She immediately started lickin' his balls gently as she massaged his dick wit' one hand and squeezed his ass wit' the other. She was runnin' her tongue up his crack and makin' circles around his booty hole which was causin' him to squirm.

"Eeew shit," Dubb said as his toes curled up. Then she pressed her face in between his cheeks and ate his booty. She was lickin' and suckin' his asshole and nibblin' on his butt cheeks. She's lickin' him the same way he licks her. "Gotdamn, you're a freaky bitch!"

"I'm your freaky bitch and don't you ever forget it!" she said, slappin' him on the ass as the music and pornos were still playin' in the background.

"Ew, I won't Cherry, I promise I won't!" Dubb exclaimed as he jumped from getting' slapped on the ass. Then, Cherry moved back to his balls and traveled down his shaft to the tip of his dick. She was bobbin' her head on it aggressively while pullin' it towards her.

"Mmmm, I want you to cum in my mouth," she said as she sucked him off vigorously from the back, smackin' him on the ass again. "What's my name?"

"Nicho.....," he got out his mouth before she spanked him some more. "Cherry!.......hell yeah bitch, I like that shit!" he said as she continued to spank him while she sucked his dick.

"Let me have it Daddy. Shoot it in my mouth," Cherry said as she literally tried to suck the nut out his dick usin' a whole lot of spit bobbin' up and down slobberin' on his Johnson.

"I'm finna shoot. I'm finna shoot. Hell yeah bitch. It's cumin, shiiiiit," he growled as his milk shot into Cherry's hot welcoming mouth. She swallowed all of it and kept suckin' and chasin' him as he squirmed away hangin' over the back of the couch. "Damn," he sighed, short of breath.

"Stop. I can't take no more," he said, runnin' from her mouth and fallin' over the couch onto the floor as they busted out laughin'.....

"I'm ready to ride your face," Cherry said, getting' the chin-strap dildo out the bag.....

"This looks like fun," she said as her and Dubb attached the sex toy around his chin. Dubb got a dildo stickin' out from his chin. He laid down on the floor as Cherry eased down on it, movin' up and down on the sex toy, poppin' her pussy, and grabbin' Dubb by the head as he licked her clit.

"What the fuck! Aw yeah, this is the shit right here!" she said, ridin' the toy and gettin' ate out at the same time. She leaned forward, puttin' all her weight on her hands and rode the shit out of Dubb's face while he licked and sucked on her clit as the dildo slid in and out of her soakin' wet pussy hole. *Damn she's wet* Dubb thought as her river overflowed onto his chin, runnin' down his neck onto his chest. *Now that's that wet-wet.........*

"Oh shit, I'm finna get it. I'm getting' it, AAAAAAAAAAAHHH SSSSHIIIITT!" she screeched as she climaxed, bustin' sweet, clear pussy cum all over him.

"Hell yeah," Dubb said getting' up not even takin' the time to take the chin-strap off. "Turn over bitch," he said, ready to fuck her from the back.

"Put it in my ass. I'm ready to give you some of this ass," Cherry said, stickin' her booty way in the air as her butthole twitched, fiendin' to get fucked.

"You sure?" Dubb asked, because she would never let him do it before. She'd turn around and fire on him every time he tried.

"Mm Hmm," I want you to have all of me. Plus, that toy felt so good in there," she said, reachin' back and grabbin' her ass, pullin' herself open for him.

He licked her from pussy her lips up to her booty hole, stickin' his tongue in it and fuckin' her in the ass wit' his tongue as he lubed himself with the sex lube. Then he raised up and gently placed the tip of his dick in her asshole.

"Oh shit, Daddy it's so fat. Take it easy baby," she said,

bracin' herself for the butt fuckin' she's 'bout to get as she felt the tip of his bull mastiff penetrate her asshole.

"Unn unh bitch. You gonna feel this dick," Dubb said, smackin' her ass, slidin' his shaft into her chocolate tunnel.

"Oh Daddy please," she whined.

"Unn uhn bitch, shut-up!" he said probin' deeper and smackin' her on the ass.

"Oh please, oh it hurts," she said, openin' her ass up even wider. "Oh, I'll take it Daddy. I'll take it like a good lil' bitch," she whimpered some more, takin' the pain wit' the pleasure as Dubb stroked her asshole at a medium pace.

"Oh Daddy, how much you got in?" she asked, whining as her asshole gripped Dubb's dick tighter than a pair of vice grips

"Half of it," he groaned as he guided himself in and out.

"Give it all to me Ryan. Let me feel all of it," Cherry said as Dubb went deeper. "Oh!" she yelled as he got all of it in and began to fuck her.

"Yes Daddy, oh yes," she said as Dubb squeezed her ass cheeks and fucked her in her ass like she's a nasty lil' whore.

"Aw yeah Cherry. I'm 'bout to skeet!"

"Yes Daddy, cum in my ass baby. Let it go deep in my asshole. Let it go baby," she said, cheerin' him on. "Fuck it baby. Aw. Fuck that ass-hole!" she rooted for him as her voice set him off like a detonator triggerin' a bomb.....

"AAAAAAAGGHH," he roared like a tiger as he exploded

deep inside her asshole.

“Shit,” they said in stereo as they collapsed on the floor, both of their chests heavin’ and movin’ up and down from lack of breath. *Shiiiit, the muh fuckaz on the pornos should’ve been watchin US!* Dubb thought to himself while Nichole was thinkin’.....*I’ll definitely keep his ass at home puttin’ it on him like that. Ain’t a bitch out there that can come behind that shit.* She don’t want her husband to want another bitch for shit. She ain’t even worried about it. She’s all over it. Ain’t enough room on that niggaz dick for another bitch.

“I’m doin’ everything I can think of to keep you happy nigga. I swear to God I’ll kill you.....”

CHAPTER 57

The next day.....

Early the next afternoon, the two "Porno Stars" woke up butt-naked, laid out on the livin' room floor. They were wore out and hung over. Nikki and Dubb stayed up fuckin' all night.....

"What you want for breakfast?" Nichole asked.

"A turkey sausage, onion and cheese omelet wit' some of those big, grand biscuits," Dubb responded.

"Mmm that sounds good. You gonna help me Mr. Nasty Man?"

"Unn unh, that's you, you lil' freaky bitch," Dubb said, laughin'.

"Pop!" Nichole smacked him 'cross the fo'head. "Watch your mouf. I'm your wife. You don't talk to me like that. Cherry ain't here right now," she said, gettin' that nigga strait.

"Oh, my bad, my bad," Dubb said, crackin' up as they headed to the bathroom to take a shower and brush their teeth before they cooked breakfast together.

After they got out the shower, Dubb cut his phones on and he had messages from everybody, Chi-Murder, Maniac, HB and J-Dogg. Bryan kept leavin' voicemails sayin' it's important and to call him back.....

"What's up bruh?" Dubb asked as his twin answered the

phone.

"What the *fuck* you been doin' nigga? I called yo' ass all day yesterday!" Bryan snapped in the phone.
"Shit nigga. I ain't know we was supposed to check in everyday. Hell, I just dropped you a mil the other day," Dubb snapped back.

"It ain't 'bout no money nigga. The feds is takin' over the investigation. I got suspended, slash forced to take a medical leave. We need to talk. Meet me at our secret hideout from when we was lil', you still remember where?"

"Yeah," Dubb responded.

"3 o'clock," then he hung up.

"Baby, what's wrong?" Nichole asked, overhearing the conversation.

"I don't know. Bryan said the Feds is takin' over the investigation. He got suspended and we need to talk. He sounds noid-n-a-bitch though. Nigga got *me* nervous."

"Well just calm down sweetie. Wait and see what he says and we'll go from there. In the meantime, let's eat. I gotta be to work in a lil' over an hour," Nikki said, glancin' at the clock headed for the kitchen...

After breakfast, they went their separate ways. Nicole went by Alexis' house to drop off some more work and to collect her money. Dubb sent her wit' 3 ½ jars of ecstasy. He kept the last 40 sum odd pills for himself and he sent her 22 ounces of cocaine. That's what was left after he sacked up the 5 ounces Nicole usually takes to the good doctor. Dubb don't want shit else in the house. He told Nichole to give Alexis the X for free and to only charge her 10 G's for the cocaine.

After he got Nikki off to work, Dubb flew out the house to grab the 79 kilos he needs for Chi-Murder and Maniac and nem'. Everybody agreed to meet up at the Bronx projects so Dubb could handle everybody in one wop cause he's short on time. This shit is crazy! Thirty bricks to Chi-Murder, another 30 to Maniac. H.B. needed 15 and J-Dogg needed 4. That's $1,185,000 Dubb made in a matter of minutes. Shit, that's damn near 1.2 million dollars. The shit's unbelievable. Them niggaz started callin' him Barack Obama. They said he's stimulatin' the economy, cause it was hard for niggaz to eat out there until he came home wit' his new plug. Now, the whole area is flooded. Them niggaz is stretchin' every brick they copped. 15 is getting' turned into 30, 30 is gettin' turned into 60. It's goin' down! Dubb hopes he makes it out the game alive and free. Everybody he's heard of that's touched big cocaine like this has either been merked or is servin' life in the feds. 68 ki's left and it's over. The way these niggaz is coppin' work, it's just one more flip.

CHAPTER 58

In the basement of the concord projects where these niggaz was raised....

"What took you so long nigga?" Bryan asked as Dubb entered the laundry room of the old projects.

"Shit, I had to wrap up some bid'ness real quick, Dubb said, slidin' him a bag filled with half a million dollars. "We even."

"Shit, that's all good. I ain't trippin' off no money. Shit's crazy. They put a FBI Agent on me. Her name was Amber Locke....

"*Was*?" Dubb cut him off.

"Yeah, *was*. The bitch had to come up missin'. She was frontin' like she was a lawyer from Baltimore who moved out here to start over after her divorce. We was fuckin' and shit and she found out too much. She knows we're brothers.

"You bullshitin'!" Dubb said in shock, gettin' mad that his brother could be so careless all while he's getting' nervous at the same time.

"Do I look like I'm bullshittin'?" Bryan asked, lookin' his twin in the face. "She found out I been stealin' a lot of shit out the evidence room for a while now. They figure I'm either killin' these snitches myself or I'm telling you who they are and you're killin' 'em," Bryan said as they locked eyes, keepin' silent far as the murders go.

"Man," Dubb sighed as it's beginning to set in that he's bein' investigated by the Feds. *One slip and it's over.*

"It's ugly bruh. After this, we gotta stay away from each other. Get whatever you got in the trap house up outta there and don't never go back. Right now, they ain't got shit on you. All your homeboys from the joint are solid. But there's some new informants that's tryin' to get close to you through them. Here's the agent's file. It's all in there," Bryan said, givin' Dubb the folder. "Look through it then burn it. If you get caught wit' it, they'll tie you to the missing agent. And keep this safe," Bryan said, givin' Dubb a key.

"I'll tell you what's up wit' it, if it's necessary," Bryan said, lookin' his brother in the eyes.

"What's in the folder?" Dubb asked.

"All her notes, theories, and information on the informants."

"Strait up?" Dubb asked.

"Fa'sho. I love you bruh. Now get the fuck outta here," Bryan said, huggin' his brother and hidin' the tears in his eyes because of not knowin' his future and wonderin' if he'll ever see his brother again.

The feds can't tie him to the murders, but they got him on a slew of charges related to all the drugs comin' up missin' from the evidence room. All thanks to the task force's evidence attendant, Charles Palmer. Amber arrested him late one night and flipped him against Bryan. Good 'ole Charlie gave a video taped statement tellin' her about all the evidence him and Bryan tampered with since 2008. Charlie agreed to set him up.

So, Bryan was on candid camera during that last transaction when he checked out those 12 ki's. All the information was right in Amber's file. Ole' Charlie's in the witness protection program livin' it up in the Rocky Mountains. All that talk of retiring early was bullshit. They can arrest Bryan at any time, but the Feds are waiting. They're tryin' to use Bryan to lead them to Dubb and tie him up in all this shit too. But so far, every link between Dubb and that cocaine has had their throat slit....

After he left from meetin' wit' his brother, Dubb went strait to the trap house and grabbed the work and threw it in Nichole's Aurora. Not knowin' what else to do, he went grocery shoppin' and drove strait to his auntie's house over on Ohio Street. Aunt Evelynn is Uncle Nook's first wife from way back in the 70's. She rode out wit' him the first 7 years of his bit, until she showed up for a surprise visit and saw a lil' high yellow bitch sittin' on Uncle Nook's lap. So Aunt Evelynn cut out. She was Bryan and Ryan's aunt when they were little, so she'll always be their aunt. Even though she divorced Uncle Nookie, she was always close by. She had other boyfriends, but none could ever compare to Big Nookie, and they've been back together the last 6 or 7 years. And now finally that he's like 58 years old, Uncle Nook 'finna come home. Just as soon as Bryan and Ryan pay 1.5 million under the table....

"Hey baybee! What brings you through here?" she said, huggin' Dubb real tight, kissin' him all over his face. "Boy, you *still* taste sweet," she said, leadin' him to the kitchen. Uncle Nook bought this house a long time ago when they first got married and had lil' Nookie. Lil' Nook got killed over in Iraq. He didn't wanna be nothin' like big Nook or the rest of the family, so he enlisted in the Marines right after high school. It's a damn shame really, cause he left Gary, tryin' his hardest to dodge a bullet and he still caught one. Servin' this country in a war tryin' to jack some fuckin' oil. He might as well stayed here jackin' dope boys wit' his family.

"What all you got in them bags sweetie?" Aunt Evelynn asked, eyein' the boxes of food, fresh fruits, and vegetables pokin' out the sacks.

"Just some groceries," he answered, givin' her "the look." Don't get it twisted, Auntie knows what time it is. Don't forget she was with Uncle Nook back in the days when he was in the game.

"Don't let me get in the way honey, go ahead and put everything away then come on back in the livin' room and keep ya auntie company for a while."

R-Dubb put the groceries up and went into the basement to stash the dope. After he came back upstairs, Dubb went into the livin' room with Aunt Evelynn to catch up on old times. He told her that they almost had the money to get Uncle Nook home, and she cried tears of joy as she told him about their plans once he gets home. As he rose to leave, Dubb let her know that he'd send a chick named Alexis over to pick up the "groceries" and Aunt Evelynn said that it was fine.

CHAPTER 59

Late Wednesday Night/Early Thursday Morning. However you wanna look at it, Club 10.....

Wednesday, nights are one of the busiest nights and the club is packed! Strippers are all over the club workin' it as "Shake That Money Maker" blasts through the speakers. Alexis is givin' this big fat ass nigga named Big Fatz a lap dance as she looked across the room seductively. She's lickin' her lips at Chico while she bends over to let Fatz rub her ass and tuck dollars in her G-string. That shit is turnin' Chico on as his lil' peter stiffens inside his Red Monkey Jeans. He knows this is her last dance for the night as he glances at his custom made Iced-out wrist watch and sees it's just a few minutes 'til 3. He figures he'll have her at the hotel buryin' his face in her lil' snatch within the next 45 minutes. After the dance, Alexis kissed Fatz on the cheek and strutted across the floor to the dressin' room as her ass followed behind her. Her booty bounced wit' every step, hypnotizin' every nigga who dared to look at it. Niggaz loved her booty so much they'd tuck dollars as she walked by. Alexis enjoyed every bit of attention she got. It made her pussy wet. She wasn't like the other strippers. That's why they didn't make money like her. The other ho's who worked at the club won't let niggaz touch 'em-n-shit. But Alexis, on the other hand, loved the feel of havin' her ass slapped and her body touched and rubbed by different pairs of hands all night. Her only rule was "tuck somethin'." If you touch her, tuck a dollar. She let's niggaz kiss her ass for 5 dollars a peck. If you got $20, she'll bend over and let you try to put a hickie on that muh fucka. At the end of the night, she sells her pussy and sweat drenched G-strings for $150.00. She never wears the same one twice. She's a star up in here and she loves it. She got dressed and sent out a text message as she put on some lipstick, lookin' in the mirror, blowin' herself a kiss and thinkin' to herself how sexy she is. She pulled out the last of her lil' sniff sack and did a couple lines and left the dressin' room. Soon as she stepped out into the club area, Big Fatz was waitin' on her. He was wavin' a hundred and fifty dollars to buy her G-string, ready to get a whiff of her sweet-n-tangy aroma. She placed her damp G-string around his neck and took the money out his hand as she kissed him on the lips.....

"What's up for the night girl? Fatz ready to spend," he said, pullin' a wad of hundreds out his pocket.

"Not tonight Big Daddy, 'nother time okay?" she said, kissin' him on the cheek before she turned to meet Chico at the bar....

"You ready Papi?" Alexis asked, struttin' up to Chico as he finished his drink.

"Ci-Ci Mami," he replied tossin' some money on the bar and takin' her hand as they walked outside the club.

They got inside Chico's white 09" Escalade sittin' on 28 inch Divincci's and pulled off the lot as Reggatone (Spanish reggae/rap music) was blastin' through the cabin of the truck....

"Hey Mami, grab me a box of Garcia Vega's and some orange juice. Get whatever you want too," Chico said, handin' her a couple twenties as he pulled up to the convenience store, right across the street from the club.

"Ok Papi, " Alexis said, gettin' out the truck.....

Alexis walked through the isles grabbin' bubble gum and candy as some old toothless muh fucka kept smilin' and wavin' at her. He was followin' her around the store and tellin' her what he would do to her if she was his...

"First thang yo' old ass need to do wit' ya lil' social security check next month is go buy you some teeth nigga! Now get ya old dusty ass the fuck out my face! You can't afford this pussy okay?" she snapped after getting' frustrated from tryin' to be nice. Old fucker couldn't take a hint.

"My bad sugar, my bad," the man tipped his hat as he backed off. "I ain't mean no harm."

These old ass niggaz is CRAZY! Alexis said to herself, poppin' her gum as she grabbed a bottle of Tropicana Orange Juice, screamin' as she dropped the bottle, bustin' it all over the floor.

Meanwhile, outside at the truck...

At the exact moment Alexis grabbed the bottle of juice, Dubb crept up to the driver's side of the Escalade...

"Pop!" the Glock .40 blasted, shatterin' the driver's side window of the truck, hittin' Chico in the shoulder.

"Put a hit out on that, you beefy bean burrito eatin' son' bitch!" Dubb yelled as Chico screamed in pain, tryin' to reach for his Nina, but it was too late....

"Pop! Pop! Pa-Pop! Pop! Pop! Pop! Pop! Pop!" the Glock blasted as Dubb squeezed the trigger 8 more times, knockin' Chico over into the passenger seat from the force of the .40 caliber slugs tearin' through his body and his face. Nothin' racial intended, but it looked like somebody smashed some tomatoes all on the interior of the Escalade. Dubb tucked the

.40 inside the pocket of his hoodie and disappeared into the night.

Alexis knew what was finna go down. She just wasn't expectin' it right then. Her and Dubb plotted the shit the other day. Alexis told him to be waitin' somewhere around the store about the time the club closed down. While she was gettin' dressed, she sent Dubb a text;

"Leavin' in 10 minutes" All Dubb had to do was wait on Alexis to get out the truck after the Escalade pulled up. That bitch should've been an academy award winnin' actress. She played the part of the grief-stricken lover to the "T". Tears, snot bubbles, passin' out and all. They had to call the paramedics over for *that* bitch! They dumb asses was checkin' her vital signs and givin' her oxygen and shit. She knew she was gonna get interviewed by the detectives and possibly searched, so she broke the cell phone and threw it away at the club. She gave a statement and was driven home by a female officer.....

Dubb made it home to find Nichole sittin' up, lookin' through the file "B" gave him earlier. Her nerves were shot from worryin' if Dubb's lil' mission would go okay.

"These bitches just rappin', tellin' everything they *think* they know about you, tryin' to set your homies up and get close to you at the same time. That's why Keisha stankin' ass was all in my face, askin' me all kinds of questions about you when she brung her baby to the hospital. I had to check the bitch. I thought she just wanted to fuck you. Now I *see* what's up and these bitches got *my* name all up in this shit," she said, mad as fuck to see people steady runnin' they mouth.

"It's all good baby. I just gotta meet my nigga 'nem one more time and we done. We won't have the 2 mill we planned on, but we'll have 1.7."

"You promise?" Nikki asked.

"I promise, and everything went ok. Don't worry," Dubb said, kissin' her on the cheek before he headed for the shower.

CHAPTER 60

2:30 p.m. Thursday…..

Dubb sat at the table in the hotel room, amazed at how much the Feds knew. They knew all about Uncle Nookie. They knew about Bryan changin' his name from Williams to Wilkins, they even know what schools he went to. They even know what type of grades the nigga got, *shit*! They knew the whole rundown on Ryan too. His arrest record, his prison records, and everything. They knew who he wrote, who wrote him, and that Nichole was the only one that came to visit. They got a lot of info on her too. Where she works, her hours, and her affiliation wit' Alexis. They know about Dubb's gang affiliation with the Renegade Vice Lords. And courtesy of the new informants, they got a lot of information on Maniac, J-Dogg, and H.B. They better be careful. H.B. don't give a *fuck*! He did 15 for shootin' the police. He got charged wit' attempted murder. Nigga tried to peel the skin off the pig's head. It looks like they checked on Chi-Murder too, but they couldn't get an informant close to him………

"Knock-knock-knock-knock-knock," Dubb got up, lookin' out the peephole to see J-Dogg and 'nem standin' in the hallway. He had to call 'em over to tell 'em what's goin' on so everybody don't get ran up.

"What's goin' down?" Dubb greeted his homies as he let them in.

"What's hap'nin?.....What it do bruh….sup bruh?" each one greeted Dubb as they exchanged daps and hugs.

"So what's really goin' on?" J-Dogg asked as everybody

sat down on the bed and at the table.

"Shiiit, you know this nigga?" Dubb asked, tossin' a picture of Da'vion Harris on J-Dogg's lap.

"Yeah, this my nigga, he Almighty, he be down in the valley all the time," J-Dogg responded.

"Fuck that nigga. That nigga ain't Almighty. That nigga the feds," Dubb said as the room got quiet. Maniac and H.B. figured he had the same type of news for them too.

"Whaaat?" J-Dogg said as his mouth dropped.

"That nigga caught a gun charge comin' back form Southbend. State boys pulled him over. He had a A.K. wit' a hundred round drum, and the pin was filed down on that bitch. The Feds picked it up cause he's a violent felon. Trigger-lock law. Long story short, they asked him could he get you and did he know who I was and he said 'yes'," Dubb explained.

"Punk muh fucka. I'll be to see him though."

"Naw bruh, don't touch him. That nigga come down wit' the cold the Feds'll be to see *you*. Just cut him off. They ain't wired him up yet. Feel me? Be careful and don't fuck wit' nobody new," Dubb said to everybody in the room.

"This bitch Kiesha?" Dubb said, handin' H.B. a picture of a sexy dark skinned chick.

"Man, how you know bou........," H.B. began.

"Just trust me Self. Cut that ho off. She the Feds. They even know what positions you fuck her in. The ho's baby daddy sent her out to New York to cop a half thang. She got popped off at O'Hare airport up in the Chi. Bitch never seen the inside of the station. She done already flipped on her baby daddy. He don't even know she got him yet. He still walkin' the streets. They wired her up and let her deliver the package. Now she tryin' to hit me through you. Look, it's all in these papers," Dubb said, handin' them the files of their informants. "I need this shit right back after ya'll flip through it. I gotta get rid of this shit."

"Man, this shit is crazy. I can't *believe* this nigga!" Maniac said as he looked at a picture of his homie from back in the days. Him and Johnte' grew up in the Miller projects together. They been runnin' mates since 1st grade. "This ho ass nigga, I thought we was family."

"Just leave them snitchin' ass bitches alone. The F.B.I. Agent that was handlin' them is umm, off the case."

"Man, how you get a hold of this shit?" H.B. asked, anxious to know. He still trippin' 'cause he thought nobody but God knew he was crashin' Keisha.

"I got a decent lil' connection, feel me?" Dubb responded, wishin' he could put 'em up on game, but he couldn't. Some things you just have to hold on your chest.

J-Dogg fired up some dro' and they sat around gettin' high, talkin' 'bout old times when they was all in the joint together. They were comparin' how they went from sittin' in the same cell block bustin' up Ramen Noodles to sittin' in a hotel room bustin' up bricks. After they left, Dubb tore the file up in tiny lil' pieces and flushed it down the toilet. Just one mo' flip and it's over……

CHAPTER 61

That Night……

"Rwock-a-bye baby on the twee top, when da wind blows da cradle will rwock, dah-ta-dah-dah-ta-dah-dah-dah-dah……," the single mother hummed and sung to her baby as she rocked in the thrift store rockin' chair, tryin' to put her child to sleep. Lil' Dae'shawn been real difficult to deal with. All that hallerin' and carryin' on all the time. He got colic. She feels guilty because she thinks it's her fault since she kept smokin' squares the whole time she was pregnant. She couldn't help it. Her nerves was bad. Dae'shawn's daddy wouldn't quit fuckin' other bitches, and when she would spazz out questionin' him about it, he'd just beat her ass. He would never give her no money to get up out her raggedy one bedroom roach motel they got the nerve to call an apartment. All that money he made, the cars, the jewelry, his nice clothes, and his plush bachelor pad, and he wouldn't give her one red cent.

"Fuck his bitch ass. Deadbeat mudder fucker. That's why I did what I did. I ain't going' to jail for that no good bastard. Ain't that right, stink-stink?" she said, rockin' her baby in her arms as she patted him on the butt.

"Good," she sighed to herself as she looked down noticing her lil' stink-stink was fast asleep. She eased out of the chair and tip-toed a couple steps to the crib cramped into the small space between the wall and the foot of the bed and laid him down inside very carefully so she don't wake his lil' hallerin' ass up. "Whew!" she breathed in relief. *Finally, peace at last,* she thought to herself as she sat back down in the rockin' chair, contemplatin' startin' her bathwater. She hates takin' baths in that nasty ass tub. All that black stuff around the cracks-n-shit. She never feels clean when she gets out.....

"You picked the wrong nigga to try to snitch on," she suddenly heard behind her as the Snitch Killer stuck her in the side of the neck with the syringe, pullin' her backwards out the rockin' chair, crashin' her to the floor. All while lil' Dae'shawn screamed and hollered from bein' jolted awake by all the commotion. The sound of her baby cryin' was the last thing Kiesha Powell, Federal Informant Number 5738 heard as she began her journey into another life.....

CHAPTER 62

About 10:00 a.m. the Next Morning……

"Aw Shit, Nikki come check out the news," Ryan yelled into the bathroom, causin' Nikki to come dashin' around the corner. She was wrapped in a towel tryin' to catch it.

"………apparently, neighbors became concerned when they heard the young child screaming all night and into the morning. They say the infant has colic and it's normal to hear him crying for extended periods of time. Eventually neighbors knocked on the door and the mother never responded. When a family member showed up at the housing project and tried to contact Ms. Powell by her cell phone, they could hear her ringtone playing inside the apartment. Fearing for the safety of the child, the victim's half-brother, Antwon Brown kicked in the door of the apartment to find the victim's body. Ms. Powell was murdered in the same fashion as the other victims. Her throat was slit, a dime was dropped on her chest, and the phrase "Speak No Evil" was written on the wall of her tiny bedroom in her own blood. At this point, it has not been confirmed that Keisha Powell was, in fact, a police informant. However, the authorities are urging anyone who has information on these terrifying murders to please come forward. Police are discouraged in their investigation. They report that residents seem somewhat satisfied in seeing the horrific murders of these quote, unquote snitches. Here's what one of her neighbors had to say. He requested that we hide his identity. The views expressed are not the views of WBN News," the reporter stated as an older heavyset black man appeared on camera with his face blurred out. "That's what the (beeeep!) gets. Do the crime, do the time. Ain't no jobs out here. The economy bad. We all out here scrapin' and scratchin', tryin' to eat. Ain't nobody got time to be worried about who's tellin'. Bet they quit snitchin' now," the unidentified man said. "This (beeeeep!) shoulda been hap'nin!"

"Wow, he obviously supports the stop snitching campaign," the reporter said sarcastically wit' a lil' snicker. "But now seriously, something must be done about these disturbing murders. This is Deborah Caldwell reporting live for WBN Channel 5. Back to the studio."

"Shit, he right though. That *is* what the bitch gets. '*Tired* of all this snitchin' goin' on. You ain't even been home a month and they got muh fuckas lined up like it's free cheese to tell on you," Nikki said. "And the bitch had *my* name in her mouth? Fuck that bitch! I feel sorry for her baby though," Nikki continued feelin' frustrated from all the pressure of worryin' about her man's future on the streets.

"C'mere girl. Quit doin' all that fussin-n-shit, and lay in the bed and sweet talk wit'cha man," Dubb said, pattin' the spot next to him.

"What 'chu wanna talk about?" Nikki asked, smackin' her lips as she laid on Dubb's chest.

"I wanna hear how much you love me," he responded.

"Boy, quit playin' You know I love you with all my heart. You're my everything, and I'm so proud to be your wife. I missed you so much while you were gone. I damn near went crazy.

"Shit, I missed you too. You the woman of my dreams. You're beautiful, sweet, sexy, smart, loyal, *and* dedicated. You held me down. You re-defined the definition of a rider. You know what my lil' nick-name for you is?"

"What?" she asked, feelin' all warm and fuzzy inside from hearin' how much Dubb appreciates her.

"Super-bitch," Dubb said, mockin' a super hero.

"Super-bitch?" Nikki asked, punchin' him in the chest.

"Ow girl, quit playin'," Dubb said, laughin'.

"Why I gotta be super bitch?" she asked, somewhat offended.

"Cause you saved the day. I mean, whenever, whatever I needed, you was *always* there. No questions, no half steppin'. You handled my lawyers-n-shit, and you kept my commissary phat wit'out me havin' to ask. The whole time I was gone, I don't never 'member havin' to ask you to send me money for commissary. I never had to stress over you, never heard about you out here givin' my pussy away. I never expected you to do everything you did and I love you for that Mommi, and I'll never forget it. Real talk, my first bit I had to put 5 bitches together to handle all the shit you did *by-your-self*! That's why I call you super-bitch. You are every hustler's dream," Dubb said as tears welled up in his eyes. Because when he thinks about all that shit, it really touches his heart. After he got caught up this time, all his bitches, his homies, and his family wrote him off for dead. But Nikki was right there from day one. She went down to that jail and swore on her life that she was gonna hold him down and she wouldn't rest 'til she got him home. And she kept her word. What they have is truly real. Unlike most couples, Ryan bein' locked up didn't tear them apart. That five year struggle helped them form a bond that could never be broken. It just brung them closer.

"Oh, I guess it don't sound too bad after all huh? I am a bad ass bitch, ain't I?" she asked, smilin' at her husband.

"Yes you are," Dubb said, kissin' her. "And let me show you how much I appreciate it," Dubb said, turnin' her over, removin' her towel, plantin' soft kisses down her stomach.

"And how you gonna do that?" Nichole asked, openin' her legs, ready for Dubb to eat her pussy.

"I'm gonna lick you 'til you cum in my mouth, then I'm gonna give you some of this dick, and then I'm gonna grill you some lemon and pepper chicken breast and fix you a salad for work," Dubb said as he parted her pussy lips, findin' her clit, gently glidin' his tongue over it as Nichole cried out in ecstasy.

CHAPTER 63

The last flip.....

After Ryan hooked Nichole up wit' lunch and saw her off to work, he hit everybody back. It's that time. They need some more dope. Everybody except J-Dogg was a lil' upset 'cause they couldn't get as much as they wanted. Tryin' to be fair, Dub agreed to sell them 20 chicks a piece, and J-Dogg would get the last 8.

Ryan knew the Feds was on him, so he was very careful. He sent everybody text messages tellin' them to send a female they trust to meet him at Willy's Pool Hall up on Broadway. He told them it's best they didn't come because it's likely they're bein' watched too. Now he just had to make a phone call real quick......

"Hello," Alexis answered, not sure who's callin' her.

"What's up wit' it girl?" Dubb responded.

"Aw shit, what's up nigga. Where Nikki at. Somethin' wrong?" she asked, catchin' his voice.

"Naw, everythang's good. I need a favor. I'll kick you out 5 G's," Dubb said.

"What you need my nigga?"

"I'll send you a text," Dubb responded then hung up. That's the new thang nowadays. Send a text instead of talkin'. If the Feds is listenin' in on they lil' frequency scanners, they could ease drop on the conversation. But, if he sent a text, they lil' equipment won't do no good.....

I need you to stop by my Aunt Evelynn's and pick up my groceries and meet me at Willy's Pool Hall Dubb typed in the phone and sent it to Alexis.

K. when? She sent back to him.

Now. He text back.

W.T.F! She sent back.

W.T.F. What is that? I don't know what all that text slang means Dubb sent back to her.

What the fuck I was kinda busy, but I got you. Where's your groceries?

521 Ohio St. She knows you comin. Dubb replied.

KTTYL she sent back

TTYL? Dubb thought to hisself. *I thought I just told that bitch I don't understand that text slang shit.*

Dubb grabbed all his money and left. He drove strait to the payphone and called himself a cab. He played them bitches. He drove Nikki's Aurora to the Concord projects and parked it out front. He got out the ride, locked the doors, and walked in the front entrance of the projects and right out the back into the cab sittin' there waitin' on him......

CHAPTER 64

...

L... THIS bitch. Dubb thought to hisself as he sipped on a double shot of Remy at his table inside the smokey ass pool hall. His ex, Brandi, came struttin' through the bar. Looks like she pickin' up some food and homegirl don't look too good either. When Dub left, she was a fine, sexy, light-brown skinned sista. Dubb kept her in the best shit. When he got locked up 5 years ago, she just disappeared. She never wrote, never came to visit, no Dear John letter or nothin'. Just vanished. They never had any um, how the chicks say it? "closure."

I came up, she went down. He thought to himself as he took another drink from his glass. *I mean, look at her, hair all over her head, shoes all wore out and turned over, mmm, mmm, mmm* he thought, shakin' his head. While Dubb was locked up, she managed to shit out two babies by two different niggaz and ain't neither one of 'em nowhere to be found. They both dogged her and cut out. *Aw shit, now here she comes.*

"Hey stranger, gimmie a hug," she said, smiling, leaning over, wrappin' her arms around Dubb as he sat at the table. "Why ain't you been to see me?"

"Why ain't you been to see *me*?" Dubb shot at her, lookin' her in the eyes as guilt instantly made her look away.

"Save that shit. You just don't understand how hard it was out here without you. I missed you so much and I will always lo......."

"Ha," Dubb laughed. "You never waited. You left me

from the gate. It's okay Brandi. It really is. I'm not mad at all. I'm really happy.

"Hmmp, I hear. I heard you married now," she said as her jaw dropped after she caught a glimpse of his iced-out weddin' band. "Got out trickin', buyin' cars and shit for that stankin' ass bitch Nikki, you need to be throwin' some of that money and some of that dick my way," Brandi said, her voice thick with envy.

"Brandi," Dubb said sippin' his drink. "Let me tell you somethin'. I could *never*, trick on my wife. I owe that woman everything I have. That girl stayed by my side for 5 years. Acceptin' my calls, sendin' me packages, keepin' commissary in my cell, comin' to see me damn near every week, and paid my lawyer's fees, while you *left*! You left me to rot in jail, runnin' 'round here throwin' your pussy away, getting' knocked up by these nothin' ass niggaz who done obviously brung you down. I ain't seen you in 5 years and you got the nerve to show up at my table disrespectin' my wife? The *only* person who stood by me. Are you crazy? Money? Throw you some money? Here, take this," Dubb said, throwin' 2 dollars on the table.

"You turned yourself into a 2 dollar ho while I was gone. Take that shit to the dollar sto' and get you a box of baby wipes, clean ya nasty ass pussy, and get back on the track. Get the fuck out my face," Dubb said as he heard a familiar laugh.

"You heard him bitch, kick rocks. He's married to *my* homegirl. Call her a bitch in her face, that's what you do," Alexis said, reachin' in her purse, wrappin' her freshly manicured fingers around her box cutter.

"Fuck you and you too. I don't need this shit," Brandi said, grabbin' her greasy bag of fish and chicken wings, headin' for the door, embarrassed and pissed off.

"You forgot your money," Alexis yelled after her as she laughed, wavin' the two dollars in the air. "Hell naw, you told her," Alexis said, laughin'.

"Naw, I was tryin' to be cool. I ain't mad at her or none of them ho's that cut out on me. I'm happy. Nikki was there. She held me down and we got really, really tight. Feel me? I ain't lettin' none of these bitches disrespect my wife."

"You really do love her don't you?" Alexis asked, takin' a seat.

""Hell yeah. I mean, why wouldn't I? She's sexy as hell, we click together, she's my best, my only friend, and what's most important to me is, she was *there*. She was there for me at a time when I really needed her. The police got everything. I had nothing. She was there when nobody else was. It's easy. Any bitch will stick by you while you out here spendin' money on her and givin' her some dick. Any nigga that wants to know which one of his chicks love him, which one he should marry, just go to jail for a minute and it will be so obvious. Nikki didn't owe me nothin'. We was only kickin' it-n-shit. We wasn't officially a couple. I'll never forget it. I told her this morning she's my 'Super-Bitch'. She saved the day. Popped up in the visitin' room one day talkin' 'bout she got me."

"Look nigga, let me tell you a secret and you better not tell that bitch I told you either. Nikki been in love wit' you from day one. She wanted to be yours from the gate. She always said when all your other lil' bitches fell off, she was gonna be the last bitch standin'. I admit it. I told her she was stupid. I wouldn't wait on *no* nigga. But, I'm glad ya'll together. I'm happy for ya'll. And ya'll muh fuckaz ever need *anything*,

anything at all, call me and I'm there. That's my fuckin' sista nigga. I love her more than I love my blood sistas. You my brother," Alexis said as tears welled up in her eyes givin' Dubb a tight hug. It really felt like the type of hug a sister would give her big brother.

"Thanks 'Lexis. You wanna drink?" Dubb said, motionin' for the waitress.

"Yeah, let me have a Belvie and cranberry juice."

The waitress came and took their drink orders doin' a double take, almost breakin' her neck to look all in Dubb's face as she took their orders. She left and came right back settin' their drinks down wit' a lil' attitude. Ryan and Alexis sat there drinkin' and talkin' about Nichole and how much they love her. They found their common thread. Today marked the beginning of their relationship as brother and sister, and it feels good. Dubb longs for a family. All of his family has either passed away or abandoned him durin' his period of incarceration. The only real family he has is Uncle Nook. Him and Nookie got pretty tight while they was at the City together. And his paternal twin Bryan? They've never been close. Bryan changed his name and moved to St. Louis in middle school. Ryan was in and out of boys school, jail, and prison. They've practically lived two completely different lives. They kinda envy one another. Each one thinks the other brother's life is better than their own. They're twins so of course they love each other, but they don't have a real brother to brother connection. Their relationship is basically bid'ness. After their drinks, they went outside and Dubb put all the work inside a duffel bag and slipped Alexis five thousand dollars as she started her car and left.

As Dubb stepped back into the pool hall, he motioned

for Willy. Willy was an old school hustler from back in the day. He used to hustle wit' Uncle Nook back then. They was ballin. The term they used back then was high rollers. All that old Willy has left from them days is his jewelry, an old 76 Fleetwood, the pool hall, and a wall full of pictures capturin' their reign at the top of the game, the fur coats, the cars, the fly clothes, and the women

"What it is youngblood?" Willy asked as he made it over to him.

"I need to use your back room to handle some bid'ness," Dubb told him.

"Now you know I gots to get my cut of anything that go on 'round here," Willy said as Dubb handed him 10 hundred dollar bills

"Well, I guess this 'bout covers it then, huh?" Willy said after he thumbed through the bills. He took off for the back room as Dubb followed behind him.

"You 'mind me of ya Uncle Nookie. All bid'ness. I sent that nigga letter 'while back. He never wrote me back. When you talk to that muh fucka, you tell him I said to kiss my ass," the old man said as he unlocked the door lettin' Dubb in the back.

"I'm expectin' a few broads to show up lookin' for me. You'll know 'em when you see 'em.

"A'ight then youngblood. I'll send 'em on back," Willy said as he shut the door

Dubb kicked back and turned on the ole' T.V. set, happy

that this is it. This is his last 'lil transaction and it's over. And right on time, the girls showed up. Each one of the homies sent a broad with the bread to make the pickup for 'em. Just to keep bullshit out of the game, Dubb had each girl call their nigga before they left to verify everything was all good. And all the homies sent a text or called to let him know the packages touched down.

After everything fell together, Dubb used the phone in the back room to call a cab to pick him up and take him to Pierre's total fitness out in Merrillville. It's a real nice fitness club where a lot of doctors and lawyers go to do cardio and aerobics-n-shit.

CHAPTER 65

Briefing at FBI Headquarters....

"This is turnin' out to be a real shit storm," SAC Montgomery said.

"Tell me about it," Mike Young, who's in charge of public relations, said as he flipped through the briefing notes. "The press is all over this mess askin' a hell of a lot of questions."

"Keep ignorin' their calls and when they do catch up with you, decline to comment. Better yet, issue a statement sayin' the informant is not one of ours. The Federal Bureau of Investigations do not handle their witnesses and informants in such careless manners," Montgomery responded.

"You want me to lie to them?" Young asked.

"Not exactly, no. Until we can consult with Agent Locke. We shouldn't divulge any information concerning her investigation. We wouldn't want to expose her or her informants," Montgomery ran off some bureaucratic bullshit, knowin' damn well he just don't want the public to know that they fucked up. Agent Locke never submitted the information on her informants to him. Montgomery don't know who they are and he can't protect them.

"What are we going to do about the Williams Brothers?" asked Agent Cartwright.

"We're waiting to arrest Bryan Williams. We have a long list of charges waiting on him. However, we aren't able to tie him directly to the murders yet. We have nothing on his brother Ryan at this time. Frankly, we're hopin' his brother Bryan will make a mistake somehow and connect us to him," SAC Montgomery explained.

"What about his wife and her friend Alexis?"

"They were to be used as step-ladders to get to Ryan. They're not important to our investigation at this time. The pressure is on us to get the Snitch Killer off the streets. Let's give it a week or so. If seargent Bryan Wilkins doesn't lead us to his brother, then we'll arrest him and charge him with what we have. The cocaine charges alone will put him away for a very, very long time," Montgomery responded.

"Who's our suspect for the murders?" Agent Young asked.

It's all suspicion and speculation at this time. There's one key common factor that we're keepin' secret for now that ties the murders together that will eventually lead us to the killer. I believe the brothers are working together, communicating with one another, and taking turns killing the informants to keep us off balance. Remember, Norman Sanders was murdered while Ryan was in prison. There's two different M.O.'s involved here. Four of the victims were injected with a powerful tranquilizer and they died from their throats being cut while they were unconscious. On the other hand, we have Candace Cain and undercover Officer Christopher Barnhill who were shot at point blank range. Ms. Cain's throat was cut post mortem. There's two killers ladies and gentlemen. One uses a gun one doesn't. My guess is Ryan is responsible for Ms. Cain and Officer Barnhill's deaths. Remember, Seargent Bryan Williams is a detective. He's no dummy. Common sense is tellin' me that he ran some kind of counter-intelligence on Agent Locke and discovered she was on to him. I believe he had her abducted. His brother Ryan was in Chicago at the time, they both have good alibis. A lil' too good if you ask me. I intend on charging Wilkins with Locke's abduction too. Now that'll be all. Everybody get to work. Let's tie somebody to these murders. Give me one piece of physical evidence and we'll make the arrest," Montgomery said dismissing his agents.

CHAPTER 66

Nikki and Dubb's house.....

Dubb was at the crib sittin' on the couch and watchin' Scarface. He was smokin' a Swisha and sippin' on Crown Royal when he heard Nikki's pipes hallerin' up the street. *Uh oh, Mommi home early* Dubb thought to hisself, happy she's home. He heard the tires screech as they came to a stop in front of the house. When he looked out the window, he noticed she didn't even take the time to park the ride as she slammed the car door and rushed towards the house. *Somethin's wrong* Dubb thought to hisself as he went to let her in the house......

"What's wrong?" Ryan asked while openin' the door and closin' it behind her.

"Fuck you, you bitch ass lyin' ass nigga!" Nicole yelled as she punched him in the mouth.

"What the.......what the fuck's wrong with you?" Ryan asked while holdin' his wife to prevent anymore blows from bein' thrown, as he tasted blood in his mouth.

"Let me go, naw nigga, let me go! I told you. I told you!" Nichole screamed at him as she cried, still tryin' to kick and punch Dubb where ever she could reach him.

"What's wrong? Talk to me, what I do?"

"So, you fuckin' Alexis? *You fuckin' Alexis?"* she asked louder the second time as her chest heaved in and out from bein' *pissed*.

"You had her and your ugly, dusty ass bitch Brandi down at the pool hall arguin' over you? Huh?" she asked at the top of her lungs as she's still strugglin' to get loose and catch her breath.

"Answer me! Don't go to sleep tonight. I told you what I'd do if you played me, didn't I?" Nichole threatened, still fightin' to get loose.

"Aw hell naw, you trippin'," Dubb said laughin'.

"Aw so it's funny huh? You think it's a joke?" she asked *really* getting' pissed, feelin' like Ryan's laughin' at her.

"*Let-me-go*! Let me go!" Nikki screamed, tryin' her best to get free from Ryan's arms.

"Will you let me explain?" Dubb asked.

"Ain't nuttin' to explain! You can't explain why I got a call at work that my *husband* was sittin' at a table wit' his raggedy ass ex-girl friend and then my supposed to be homegirl shows up and them bitches started arguin'. Then you and Alexis's whorish ass was sittin' there havin' drinks makin' goo-goo eyes at each other. You can't explain that shit. You think I'm bullshittin' don't you? You better not *ever* let me up. Don't let me up," Nichole threatened, cryin' and out of breath.

"Baby, you need to calm down, it wasn't even like that at all. You need to go check whoever broke they neck to tell you that bullshit. I love you girl and Alexis do too. We wasn't on no bullshit," Dubb explained, tryin' to calm her down.

"Yeah ya'll was. What was you doin' at the pool hall wit' your ex and why was they arguin'?" Nikki asked, wrestlin' and tryin' to get loose.

"I was waitin' on Alexis, and Brandi came and sat at my table, hatin' on us and our marriage. She was callin' you a bitch-n-shit. So I checked her. I called her a two dollar ho and threw a couple bucks at her. Then I told her to leave my table. I guess 'Lexis overheard the shit and Brandi wasn't movin' fast enough so Alexis checked her too. You trippin'," Dubb explained.

"What the fuck was you waitin' on Alexis for?" Nikki demanded to know.

"Look baby, can I let you go now, are you cool?" Dubb asked sweetly as he looked into her eyes.

"Do what you wanna do," Nichole said.

"Girl, don't start trippin'!" Dubb said, turnin' her loose as she immediately started swingin' on him all wild-n-shit.

"Fuck you! What was you waitin' on Alexis for?" Nikki screamed as she punched Dubb in his chest and all over his shoulders.

"Look, you know the Feds on us. I had the work stashed over Uncle Nook's house. I had Alexis pick it up and bring it to me at the pool hall. Here, look in my phone, look at the text messages," Dubb said, givin' her his cell phone.

"We done, all the work is gone," Dubb continued as Nichole flipped through the text messages. Seein' that Dubb was tellin' the truth. She tossed the phone on the couch and mushed him in the face.

"Damn, what was that for? I told you the truth."

"Pull ya dick out," Nikki ordered with her hand out.

"What?" Dubb questioned.

"You heard me. Pull your dick out I wanna smell it. It better not smell like soap and it better not smell like pussy. That muh fucka better smell like you been sittin' on your musty ass balls all day," Nichole said with her arms folded and her lips twisted lookin' Dubb dead in the eyes. She was waitin' on him to comply with her order.

"Damn girl," Dubb said, unzippin' his jeans and reachin' in his draws to present himself for inspection. Nichole gripped his dick, sniffin' it and lookin' at it, givin' it a thorough examination. Satisfied that everything appears okay, she squeezed it tight as she could.....

"Ow girl, shit! Why you – you squeezin' my dick?" Dubb asked as he hopped tryin' to fee himself from her grip.

"Let me tell you somethin'. You are not to *ever* call Alexis' phone again. That's *my* homegirl, not yours. Both ya'll some ho's, and ho's and alcohol equals sex. You are not to meet *no* bitch, *no* where for nothin'! If you felt like you needed Alexis to pick your shit up, you should've called me, then I would've called her. You understand?" Nichole said, throwin' Dubbs' dick down like it was an old raggedy dish towel or somethin'.

"Baby c'mere," Ryan said, reachin' for her with one hand and rubbin' his dick with the other.

"Naw, get off me," Nichole said, snatchin' away from him. "Don't do this to me," she said, sittin' on the couch as tears fell

down her face."I've put my all into you. I waited on you. I did everything a real bitch 'posed to do and then some. I can't have you fuckin' around on me. I ain't goin' for that shit. I love you, but I swear to God I'll kill you."
"But I didn't do shit," Dubb responded as he sat down next to her on the couch. "Look at me," he said, turnin' her face towards his.

"Don't....touch me!" Nichole said, snatchin' her head away as she balled up her fist. "That's the whole point. You ain't did shit and you got me trippin' like this. I love you too much. That's the problem. You'll never under*stand* how much I love you. Look, I need a drink. I'm finna go for a ride to clear my head. I'll be back," Nikki said, gettin' off the couch and pickin' up her purse and her keys off the floor. "I love you. I'll be back in a lil' while," she said openin' the door.

"I love you too," Dubb said as he thought to himself *This bitch crazy.*

CHAPTER 67

Behind the old Hook's drug store.....

"It's two for thirty, not 29.99, 24.99, 25, 28 or none of that shit. Thirty, you hear me? Don't come to me short no mo'," the hustler said as he sold the fiend some crack in the dark alley right off of 5th Avenue and Jackson Street. The poor old crack fiend only had $26 and some change. *I hate havin' loose change in my pockets* homie thought to himself as he posted up against the back of the buildin', smokin' a square, waitin' on his next "sting". It's Friday and it's been crankin' all day.

"Sup man, you got a fifty?" another crackhead asked as he approached. Homie didn't say a word. He just exhaled cigarette smoke as he reached in his pocket and handed the crackhead 3 rocks as he took the 2 twenties and a ten that was balled up inside the dope fiend's fist.

Tonight's a good night and it's gettin' better he smiled to himself as mean Geraldine Elkins strutted up the alley. Ole mean Geral*dine*! She used to be a bad bitch back in the days. She's mixed, her daddy was black and Indian and her momma was Creole. Geraldine was light and bright, damn near white. She had green eyes and that long silky black hair. She looked like a movie star back in the fifties. She was the highest paid ho out there on the stroll. Couldn't no other bitch touch her. She used to whore for Richard "Pretty Dick" Jackson back in the day. Her and Pretty Dick used to get money all *over* the Midwest. I mean Milwaukee, Detroit, Toledo, Cincinnati, Chicago, and everywhere in between. They'd always come back to the "G". It was their home. Geraldine and Pretty Dick used to snort powder all day everyday but when crack hit in the late 80's, it was all over. They got hooked and fell off, they lost it all. They had nice cars, clothes and houses, all paid for by Geraldine's *mouth*. Most whores bragged that their *pussy* was lined wit' gold. The story goes, that after Geraldine made Pretty Dick his first half million dollars, he had every single tooth in her mouth plated wit' 24 karat gold and laced the front 12 wit' diamonds. These niggaz runnin' around here can't *touch* her grill and her shit was done back in the 50's. Her pussy wasn't the main attraction, it was that whore's mouth. Geraldine could suck a *mean* dick. That's how she got her name. They say the bitch got mo' power in her jaws than a 180 horsepower vacuum compressor. Bitch'll make you skeet faster than a 14 year old lil' boy gettin' his first shot of pussy.....

"Hey daddy," Geraldine said as the dim light in the alley reflected off her teeth. "Mean Geraldine need a hit," she said as she strutted up to him, pullin' him out the light over to the side of the dumpster.

He already know what time it is. Geraldine ain't bought no dope off him in two years. Niggaz won't admit it, but she sucks all the dope boys dicks from 5th Avenue, all the way up to 46th Street. She ain't waste no time. She reached into her oversized pocket book, threw her knee pad on the ground, whipped that niggaz dick out and went to work! *In-that-order*. Her head was bobbin', drivin' the nigga wild as he struggled to stay on his feet. Geraldine's head will make the *strongest* nigga weak in the knees. You really need to lay down to let this bitch suck yo' dick.

"Aw shit," he moaned out loud as he closed his eyes, leanin' against the dumpster, holdin' her head. "Aw *hell* yeah!" he moaned again as she started rubbin' his balls while she put pressure on tip of his dick wit' her lips and flicked her tongue across the head. He's doin' his best not to blow a hole in the back of her throat from skeetin'. He's tryin' to get his money's worth, but he don't think he can hold on much longer as she dropped his pants around his ankles and really went to work.

"Aaawww fuck!" he said, explodin' in her throat, loosin' his balance while somethin' sharp stabbed him in the neck as he collapsed to the pavement...

"Keep your head down bitch, don't fuckin' look up," the Snitch Killer said with the gun pointed at the expert dick sucker's head.

"I'm cool honey, this Geraldine. I ain't made it out here on these streets 54 years tellin' what I see," she said like it ain't nuttin'. She's witnessed more than a few murders in her day.

"Look bitch, shut the fuck up!" the Snitch Killer said, tryin' to decide whether to kill this ho or not.

"Pull that syringe out that niggaz neck and drop it on the ground," the Snitch Killer said. Geraldine did as she was told. "Good girl," now go through all that niggaz pockets, get all his money and all his dope," the killer said as Geraldine started rummagin' through the hustler's pockets as he laid unconscious.

"Okay sugar, I got it! I got all his shit," Geraldine said, holdin' it out for the killer.

"Naw, you keep it, put it in your pockets and get the fuck outta here," the killer said, wavin' her away wit' the gun.

"Thank you, thank you so much baby, you won't be sorry. unn uhn honey. Mean Geraldine ain't seen nothin'" she said, puttin' the sack full of dope in her bag along wit' his bank roll as she rose off her knees to walk away. After the Snitch Killer thought about it……

"Thwp, thwp, thwp," the silenced pistol whispered as three 9 millimeter slugs tore through the whores face and chest.

Fuck that, this ho's DNA is all over this niggaz dick. Soon as they run some tests, they'll be right at her. Bitch ain't finna tell on me. Ain't nobody gonna shut they mouth and take a murder case that ain't theirs….

CHAPTER 68

Nikki and Dubb's.....

"Where you been?" Nichole asked, sittin' on the couch wit' her legs curled up under her as Dubb walked in the house.

"I went to grab a sack real quick," he replied, takin' off his coat and sittin' on the couch next to her. He was gettin' ready to roll a Swisha.

"I brung you some fried smoked sausages and onions from Jim's if you hungry. I got you some onion rings too."

"For real?" Dubb said as his face lit up. He loves Jim's deep fried smoked sausages.

"Oh, and I bought you a box of Cigarillo's while I was at the liquor store."

"Thanks baby," Dub said as he started to get up and head for them sausages.

"Hold on," Nikki said, takin' his hand. "Look baby, I'm sorry about all that shit earlier. You just gotta understand where I'm comin' from. I waited on you for *five* years while all these bitches was runnin' around here laughin' at me and callin' me stupid and crazy. I sacrificed everything for you. I gave you everything I had. I just want to prove everybody wrong about us. They all said that you was gonna get out and keep fuckin' all these bitches like you been doin'. Then I'm at work mindin' my bid'ness and I get a message at the nurses station to call Sylvia on my next break....

"Hold on, that's the bitch that was starin' and lookin' at me all funny-n- shit," Dubb said, cuttin' her off.

"Yeah, she works down there, so I called her back and she tells me that *my* husband was down at the pool hall and Alexis and your ex was fightin' over you. I just lost it when she said Alexis ran Brandi off and you and Alexis sat there havin' some drinks. It really fucked me up. I hope you understand. I'm really sorry. I just gotta learn to trust you more," Nikki said wit' cute lil' puppy dog eyes as she apologized. "My bad, I should've known her old gossipin' ass was just tryin' to start some shit."

"It's all good boo-boo. You just gotta understand that I truly appreciate everything you done for me. You were the *only* one there for me. I'd never play you—*never*. You brung me home, ain't no way. Til' death do us part. I'm loyal to you forever. And 'Lexis? That's your homegirl. That bitch was gettin' ready to slash Brandi's face for callin' you a bitch. And them drinks? We sat there talkin' about you. 'Lexis was tellin' me how real you are, how you was always there for her since kindergarten. She admitted how she was trippin' on you for puttin' your life on hold for me. But she says she ain't never seen you so happy and she's glad we're together. That's when she gave me a hug."

"I feel really bad. Can I have a kiss?" Nichole asked, leanin' in towards his lips.

"Nope, you don't know how to act," Dubb joked wit' her.

"Boy, you better *give* me a kiss," Nikki said as she tackled him on the couch, layin' on top of him.

"I love you daddy, I'm sorry, ok? I promise I'll be good,"

Nikki said before she kissed him passionately, trying to transfer every feeling she has in her heart for him through her tongue as they laid locked in a warm embrace, intensely explorin' each other's mouth as they began to undress each other. Their kiss stirred the type of burnin' sensation deep down in the pit of their stomachs that can only be ignited by two people who are truly in love with each other.....

CHAPTER 69

Bryan's Crib, Southside Chicago.....

"Aw yeah baby, right there, just like that," Sasha said as she rode Bryan's mouth, grindin' her sweet lil' pussy over his tongue in a sensual rhythm.

"Mmm hmm," he moaned in pleasure, enjoyin' her sticky serum as Sasha's friend Vida gripped his dick tightly in her fist, lickin' the head and movin' her tongue around it in circles while she jacked him off. These bitches bad too. Sasha's a thick curvaceous chick wit' a light caramel complexion. She has nice perky lil' B-cup titties with dark chocolate nipples that look like lil' Hershey Kisses and nice long sandy brown hair. Her friend Vida's a hot mamacita with long silky black hair and full D-size titties, wit' dark sexy eyes. They all in Bryan's master bedroom butt-naked gettin' it on.....

"Oooh papi, you feel so good," Vida said in her sexy Spanish accent as she slid down on Bryan's pole, gyrating her tight lil' kitty cat round and round, buckin' on his dick, and touchin' all the right spots inside her pussy as she moaned in pleasure.

Sasha, curious and wantin' to watch her friend ride some dick, turned around and sat on Bryan's face backwards. Sasha was entranced by Vida's titties bouncin' as she hopped up and down on Bryan's dick. Vida would sit all the way down and ease slowly all the way to the top, takin' her time, getting' every inch of it. Not able to watch any longer, Sasha leaned forward and began to suck and massage Vida's titties as all three of them cried and yelled out in pleasure.

"Ooh shit, its' cumin' papi, ew papi, my pussy is cummmmmmming!" Vida cried out while her pussy contracted around Bryan's shaft in spasms as her body jerked. Unable to take anymore, Vida rolled off Bryan's dick and laid on the side of him as she watched Sasha get ate out.

"Mmm hmm, put your fingers in my pussy," Sasha ordered as she continued to hump Bryan's face.

"Oh yes! Hell yes!" she exclaimed as Bryan shoved two fingers in her moist snatch and began finger fuckin' her. Sasha, lookin' down at his black slippery dick became anxious to taste Vida's pussy. So, she grabbed it and took him in her mouth savorin' the mixture of cum and pussy juice. She sucked him off vigorously as his fingers probed in and out of her wet pussy while his tongue danced all over her clit. They kept lickin' and suckin' each other until they released their juices in each other's mouth. Bryan playfully slapped Sasha on the ass as she got off his face. He quickly glanced at the T.V. monitors enclosed in an oak cabinet installed along his bedroom wall. Then he rolled over and took another swig of Hennessy and cut a few more lines of powder for him and the girls to give them a lil' kick to keep their fuck fest goin'. Bryan ain't been doin' shit but getting' wasted, and fuckin' and suckin' every bitch he can every since he realized the Feds got him.

Bein' a task fore detective, he has a wide variety of surveillance equipment. His place is completely surrounded with high tech cameras that can transmit visuals in light or darkness. *If them bitches are comin', I'll be ready* he thought to himself as he eyed the M-16 sittin' on the floor next to the bed and the uzi layin' on the nightstand. There's a fully automatic weapon within arms reach anywhere in his house. Some would say he's paranoid. He says he prepared. He knows they're comin', he just don't know when. He has a state of the art scanner/scrambler that will pick up any radio or cell phone frequency within miles of his house. He'll hear them bitches comin', settin' up their perimeters way before they get there. You can't run from the Feds, and he knows it. And prison ain't the place for a cop whether he's dirty or not. He just shrugged his shoulders to hisself and said *fuck it* and sniffed the long line of powder he just cut up on his nightstand.

CHAPTER 70

The next mornin'.....

"Read this shit," Dubb said, droppin' a newspaper on the bed just getting' back from pickin' him and Nikki up a box of caramel rolls and some chocolate milk from Vogels....

Gary Tribune

The mysterious Snitch Killer has struck again! Late Friday night, the bodies of Geraldine Elkins (54) and suspected Federal informant Johnte' Cambell (29) were found in the alley behind the old Hook's Drug Store off Jackson Street. Mr. Cambell was murdered in the same fashion as the other informants. His throat had been slashed from ear to ear. The killer dropped a dime on his chest and wrote the phrase, "Speak No Evil" on the side of the dumpster next to the victim's body. Federal investigators report that apparently Cambell was receiving oral copulation from Ms. Elkins as they were attacked. The medical examiner's report states that Ms. Elkins died from a single gunshot wound to her face and two gunshot wounds to her chest, one striking her in the heart. Due to alleged corruption within the local law enforcement agencies, the FBI has taken over the investigation. Field Agent Michael Young released a statement denying the last two victims were FBI informants, stating, "The Federal Bureau of Investigation does not handle their witnesses and informants in such careless manners." The agent declined to comment much further. However, he did say that investigators now believe there are two killers.

"Who the fuck they think is doin' this shit?" Nichole asked.

"You already know. I hallered at Bryan the other day and he told me they think it's either me and him or one of us payin' somebody," Dubb said, takin' a big ole bite of his caramel roll then washin' it down with ice cold chocolate milk."

"Aw shit, *hell* muh fuckin' naw," Nichole said, crackin' the fuck up. "Listen to this shit."

"Late Friday night, local stripper Ayzia A'Jumu was arrested for residential entry, domestic battery, felony assault, resisting arrest and felony battery on a police officer. The arrest stems from an incident last night where A'Jumu went to the home of her husband's mistress. Police reports state that Mrs. A'Juma received a tip that her husband was over another woman's house on her Twitter page. Upon arriving at Tiffany Guerro's home at 3644 E. Hayes, Mrs. A'Jumu peeked in the bedroom window and witnessed her husband and Ms. Guerro having sex. Mrs. A'Jumu then broke into the residence and beat Guerro and her husband Shaheim A'Jumu repeatedly with a tire iron causing injuries and lacerations to the victims of the attack. When officers responded to the 911 call, Mrs. A'Jumu was chasin' her husband throughout his mistresses house striking him with the tire iron. Uniformed officer Ronald Wolfe was also struck with the tire iron and suffered several bite marks and abrasions from Mrs. A'Jumu as he made the arrest. Officer Wolfe was treated and released at the scene. At press time, Ms. Guerro was hospitalized and ironically within an hour of the incident, Mr. A'Jumu posted $45,000 bond for his wife and she was released and awaiting trial.

"Hell naw," Dubb said as him and Nichole bust out laughin'.

"Watch this, I'm 'bout to log on to this bitch's page,

Nichole said, loggin' on....

"Look, look, I told you," Nichole said, pointin' to the screen and showin' Dubb that Ayzia got to 327 mentions on Twitter already and it's still morning. "Hell naw baby, look at her Tweet." Nikki said, readin' out loud.....

It's all good bitch. That's why he's gonna be eatin' my pussy all night tonight trick.

Ayzia tweeted that shit along wit' a link the newspaper article and her mug shot. That shit's crazy. Bitches from all over the world is respondin' to this shit.....

Keep that mother fucker in check," a chick from Africa named Kenya008 tweeted.

You should've beat the bloody cunt whore to death! Outbackbtich82 from Australia responded in a mention to Ayzia. The tweets went on and on. Bitches from England, Canada, Brazil, Indonesia, Japan and Italy. Bitches was respondin' from all over the globe. Hell naw!

"Let me call Alexis and see what's goin' on," Nichole laughed as she dialed the number.

"What's up bitch?" Alexis answered.

"What the fuck happened wit' Ayzia and 'nem? I just saw the paper." Nichole asked

"Girl, both them bitches crazy. They upstairs. They ain't even been to sleep yet. Ayzia been beatin' his ass all night." They gettin' on my damn nerves, shit........

The girls continued to talk on the phone as Dubb crashed about 3 or 4 caramel rolls. They got to gossipin' about some of everything. Nicole even told Alexis how Sylvia called her and had her snappin' out over that bulllshit. They stayed on the phone for what seemed like an hour until Dubb made her get off the phone. They got a long day ahead of them. Today they're goin' to the big aquarium up in Chicago and then they goin' to Gibson's steak house. It's a famous steak house where all the stars eat when they in the Chi. Nichole plans on gettin' a lil' shoppin' in too. They plan on bein' back in Gary befo' it gets too late. If Nicole plans on gettin' it all in, she better hurry up.

CHAPTER 71

Late Saturday Night......

It's been crankin' down here in the valley. Da'Vion been servin' cluckers on the corner and hoppin' in and out of cars one after another all night. It's amazin' how these ho ass niggaz be certified snitches, but be out in the hood still tryin' to hustle, frontin' like they solid-n-shit.

"Woo-eeeee!" Da'Vion yelled, flaggin' down a white couple in a 90 sumthin' Chrysler New Yorker. "Make a block," he instructed as he got in the back seat of the dusty, stale smellin' car.

"We need a fifty," the man said as they pulled off.

The key is silence when you out there hustlin' like this. You gotta hope it's not a set-up and pray the task force don't rush the car from all directions, catchin' you with a sack of dope and some marked money.

Hunh," Da'Vion said while handin' the skinny white lady 3 stones over the seat as he took the money.

"Aw yeah, this is fat, look babe," the chick said, showin' her husband the rocks.

"Oh Yeah! That's fatter than what we been gettin'. If you don't mind, we just wanna deal with *you* from now on. What's your name partner?" the man asked lookin' at Da'Vion in the rearview mirror as Da'Vion sat silent......

"We're not the cops bud. I'll prove it to you. You like

gettin' head?" The man asked lookin' Da'Vion in the eyes through the rearview mirror.

"Huh?" Da'Vion asked, kinda thrown off guard.

"Do you like head? I'll pull over in that alley over there and let my lil' darlin' right here suck you off, ain't that right hun?"

"Yeah baby, don't be shy," the lady said, turnin' around in her seat, smilin' and showin' a set of black rotten ass teeth as she patted Da'Vion on the leg. He was thinkin' about it at first, but that killed it right there.

"I'm cool, just let me out right here," he said, pointin' to the curb as the crackhead pulled over.

"What's ya name bud?" the man called after him as he got out the car. Da'Vion completely ignored him and didn't even look back as the New Yorker pulled off. And no sooner than the New Yorker's tail lights disappeared around the corner. An older model rusted out Buick Regal pulled up.

"You workin?" the driver called from the car.

Da'Vion nodded his head and looked both ways then ran around to the passenger door and got in as the car pulled off.

"Aw shit. Gotdamn! What the fuck you got in this raggedy muh fucka?" Da'Vion said, liftin' up out the seat and rubbin' his ass as he felt a sharp burnin' sensation.

"Muh fucka, what the...? Muh fucka you got needles and shit in this bitch! I hope you ain't got A.I......."Da'Vion managed to get out his mouf before he slumped back down in the seat...

CHAPTER 72

The Next Morning WBN News Channel 5……

"City council members, government officials, and law enforcement agencies are in an outrage this morning. The body of 33 year old Da'Vion Harris was found on the lawn of the Lake County Courthouse early this morning. He was found inside this older model Buick Regal you see parked behind me. As you can see, detectives are converged at the scene processing the vehicle in hopes of finding *any* kind of physical evidence leading them to the killer. So far, the Snitch Killer has been very careful in not leaving any evidence behind. Law enforcement officials are very aggravated at this arrogant and defiant act on behalf of the Snitch Killer. It appears the killer is taunting them, laughing in their faces, and sending them a message. Harris was found in the same nearly decapitated state as the other victims. The killer dropped a dime in his lap and wrote, "Speak No Evil" on the windshield of the vehicle. Hol,..hold on, here comes one of the investigators now….."

"Sir, sir do you have any suspects?" Deborah Caldwell asked, holding the microphone to the detective's mouth trying to keep in step with him as he's obviously trying to get away from her.

"No comment," Agent Young responded.

"Did you receive any evidence at the scene?" Deborah asked, struggling to keep up with the detective in her heels.

"*No* comment," the agent said more forcefully this time as he got into the tactical van.

"Will an arrest be made soon?"

"Excuse me ma'am we have work to do," the agent said sliding the door shut in the news reporter's face.

"Not many words from a disgruntled detective. This is Deborah Caldwell reporting live for WBN Channel 5."

CHAPTER 73

About An Hour and a Half Later.....

"Alpha 1, this is Delta team approaching target residence, ETA 5 minutes."

"Radio once you reach the rendezvous point," Alpha 1 responded.

I guess it's showtime Bryan thought to himself when he heard the radio traffic. He hit the send button on his cell phone to transmit the text he had saved in drafts just for this occasion. Then he broke the phone and ground it in the garbage disposal.

Shit he said to himself, reachin' behind the refrigerator, grabbin' the AR-15, and headin' to the hall to get his bullet-proof vest.

I hope ya'll ready to play Bryan said to the Feds even though they couldn't hear him as he opened the hall closet and slid the bullet-proof vest over his head and fastened the straps. He quickly scanned the shelves and snatched a couple boxes of ammunition for the AR and a Glock .45 wit' 2 extra clips. He shut the hall closet and took a long guzzle of the Jack Daniels Whiskey that was sittin' on the table in the hall.

Let's do it he said as the jack made his body shiver. He cut the hall light out and headed for the basement......

CHAPTER 74

Meanwhile……

"That breakfast was off the hook," Nichole said, thinkin' about the breakfast they just had at the pancake house.

"Baby, hand me my cell phone real quick," Dubb said, hearin' his text alert as they sat on the couch flippin' through channels on the T.V.

"Here you go sweetie," Nikki said, getting the cell phone off the end table and handing it to him.

"Damn, what the…….," Dubb said, stoppin' midsentence while readin' the text message.

"What's wrong baby, what's it say?" Nikki asked, becomin' concerned.

The key. U-Stor Self-Storage in Merrillville. Lot 4606 F. They're comin' for me, watch the news Dubb read the text. "Sounds like that nigga in trouble. Fuck!"

"Don't you think you should call him?" Nichole asked as she flipped to channel five catchin' the end of a commercial.

"Nah, he told me we had to stay away from each other," Dubb said while erasin' the text, hopin' everything turns out o.k.

"Uh oh baby, look at this shit," Nichole said while turnin' the T.V. up as the news came back on…..

"This is Deborah Caldwell reporting live outside Detective Bryan Wilkins' suburban estate on the outskirts of Chicago's southside. Detective Wilkins is also known as Bryan Williams, nephew of the notorious cop killer Ned "Nookie" Williams and brother of convicted drug dealer and gang member Ryan "R-Dubb" Williams. The detective is wanted as a person of interest in the mysterious snitch killings. He's also wanted for conspiracy to murder and kidnap Federal Agent Amber Locke, as well as a long list of charges including official misconduct, conspiracy to distribute cocaine, continuing a criminal enterprise and evidence tampering stemming back from May of 2008. Right now, as you see, we're standing at the edge of the property line. The FBI as well as local law enforcement has the house surrounded. They are currently attempting to establish communication with the suspect. Their intelligence tells them that he is inside. He has not been spotted leaving the residence. FBI spokesperson, Agent Michael Young, has stated that if the suspect does not respond within the next couple of minutes, they will force entry. We'll be live, right here on Channel 5, WBN News covering the action as it unfolds.....

CHAPTER 75

The raid.....

"........go ahead and force entry," S.A.C. Montgomery ordered as Alpha 1 picked up his radio.

"This is Alpha 1. Bravo and Charlie teams standby for go. I repeat standby. Delta team hold your positions and wait for further instructions. Go! Go! Go!," Alpha 1 commanded and instantly the windows of the house burst from suppression grenades being fired as the front and back entrances to the house were knocked in by battering rams. The house was overcome with smoke as two dozen agents stormed the residence running room to room searching for any sign of their suspect.....

"Bravo to Alpha, all clear," Bravo 1 reported.

"Copy Bravo team, Charlie team?" Alpha responded, waiting on the status of the suspect.

"Charlie team clear, no sign of the target."

"Delta team, enter and initiate the search. I want it combed from top to bottom. Alpha team stand down," Montgomery instructed as Alpha team patiently held their positions outside the perimeter, fingers resting on their trigger guards, aiming their sniper rifles at every window and doorway of the house awaiting further instruction......

"Let's go!" Special Agent Montgomery ordered as he ran towards the house behind Delta Team with his radio in hand.

CHAPTER 76

Meanwhile……

Run nigga, run!!! Bryan was runnin' towards the edge of the woods, feelin' like one of the runaway slaves who escaped through the very tunnel he just ran through over a hundred-sixty years ago. His house used to be part of the 'Underground Railroad' that smuggled runaway slaves from the deep south all the way up north and sometimes into the west. He felt relived as he approached the old Ford Explorer he had hidden under some brush and threw his AR-15 inside. He got in the Explorer and put on the old Rastafarian dread lock wig and red, black and green toboggan cap he used to wear on some of his undercover operations. He started the truck and threw on his dark aviator sunglasses glancin' at his watch as he drove off. *One minute* he thought to himself as his property grew smaller in his rearview mirror……

CHAPTER 77

Nikki and Dubb's.....

At the same time, Nicole and Ryan sat glued to the T.V. with their mouths hung open.....

"We just got word that the suspect is not inside the residence," the news reporter stated.

"Aw my God, thank you," Nichole exhaled, grabbing her chest as Ryan yelled, "hell yeah, that nigga *slipped* they muh fuckin' asses!"

"........we are standin' by as Federal Agents search the suspect's residence for further evidence linking him to conspiring or participating in the snitch killings as well as a long list of other state and federal violations. This is Deborah Caldwell WBN live on Channel 5 bringin' you an exclusive look. We'll report back with more as the story unravels."

CHAPTER 78

All The While……

“I want everything, hair off his hairbrushes, collect his sheets, see if we can find any DNA or blood samples linking him to agent Locke,” Montgomery barked as he stepped over papers and clothes the agents were dumping on the floor as they conducted the search.

“Where the fuck is Young and Cartwright?” Montgomery growled as he stomped through the house.

“They’re in the basement sir,” one of the agents responded as he rummaged through the hall closet. “That way, then turn to your left,” the agent direct as he continued going through Bryan’s shit.

“C’mon, c’mon, c’mon, there has to be *somethin’* in here,” Montgomery snapped as he headed down the stairs.

“It’s a bomb! It’s a bomb! Everybody out!” Agent Cartwright screamed into his walkie talkie as him and agent Young ran up the stairs, bumpin’ into Agent Montgomery……

CHAPTER 79

At That Very Moment.....

"Oh my God," Nichole said, droppin' her jaw.

"What the f.....," Dubb said at the exact same time as they saw Bryan's house explode, collapsin' to the ground in front of them on the T.V. screen. Deborah Caldwell's lil' pretty self fell and broke one of her heels as the picture jarred and shook. Evidently, the cameraman fell from the pressure of the blast. "Hell naw, that nigga blew *all* them bitches up!" Dubb said laughin', clappin' his hands and rootin' for his brother. And then....

Boom!

"Aw, shit!" Dubb yelled as their front door suddenly flew open with Homicide Detectives Craig Garner and Drew McPherson runnin' up in the house with a gang of uniformed officers behind 'em.

"Freeze, don't fuckin' move, put your hands up!" Detective Garner yelled at the couple entering their livin' room wit' his gun drawn as Nichole screamed in panic, startled by her house bein' filled wit' cops.

"What the fuck ya'll want? I ain't did shit," Dubb said as him and Nichole were dragged off the couch and thrown to the floor.

"Get the fuck off my wife! You bitches better not hurt her. Here I go right here. She ain't did shit, leave her alone!" Dubb cussed at the cops as he tried to struggle to his feet to defend his wife.

"You don't know your wife too good then do you?" Drew McPherson butted in, pullin' out a set of handcuffs.

"Nichole Williams, you're under arrest for the murder of Detective Cristopher Barnhill and an additional 8 counts of murder, 2 counts of abuse of a corpse and 4 counts of obstruction of justice," Detective Garner said, runnin' off the list of charges as Ryan gazed at his wife in disbelief. It seemed like the room started spinnin' around as Dubb's heart sunk to the pit of his stomach.

Hell naw, ain't no way Dubb thought to himself in shock as they put the handcuffs on Nichole and read her her rights. She doesn't even look surprised. It looks like she was expectin' this shit and it's scarin' the hell out of him.

"Everything's gonna be okay baby," Nichole said as tears fell from her face. "I love you, I….."

"Shut up!" Dubb yelled, cuttin' her off, scared that she was gonna say somethin' stupid like she did it cause she loved him. "Just shut the fuck up, you hear me? Don't you say one more muh fuckin word. Don't talk to these bitches. Don't say shit! Keep your *fuckin*-mouth-shut! I'm gettin' you a lawyer mommi, you hear me? I'm gettin' you a lawyer!' Dubb yelled as his eyes welled up with tears, hurt at the thought of losin' Nichole, but touched by the notion that she's killed for him over and over. *I hope she knows it. I'm gonna hold her down the same way she did me.*

"Alright, alright, alright, enough legal advice Mr. Cochran," Garner said as they led her out the house with her head down.

"Soon as they start askin' you questions, ask for a lawyer," Dubb screamed after her as she left.

"You need to go have a seat in the kitchen. We have a search warrant and we're going to be a while," McPherson said, guidin' Ryan to the kitchen table.

"Cigarette?" McPherson offered as he pulled one out for himself. Dubb waved him off, shakin' his head no as he sat at the table with a disgusted look on his face.

"Where was your wife last night. Were you with her?" McPherson asked as he set a small recorder on the table.

"Look man, you can just shut the fuck up talkin' to me right now. You *know* I ain't sayin' *shit*," Dubb said, muggin' the detective, knowin' that if he attempts to give Nichole an alibi, it could hurt her if she says somethin' different. He hopes she don't say nothin' at all.

"Okay, I tried to be your friend."

"Fuck friends and fuck you too. Do what you gotta do then get the fuck out my house," Dubb said, still locked on the detective's eyes.

"Have it your way tough guy," McPherson said, frustrated as he rose from the table.

"Hey guys, come look at this shit," one of the detectives said with a laugh. "Look at these dildo's," the detectives said, tossin' the double action dildo at the rookie detective.

"Eeew!" the detective said, getting hit in the head by the

rubber dicks as he tried to dodge it, causin' the room full of detectives to laugh.

Punk muh fuckaz Dubb thought to himself, pissed and embarrassed that these bitches is in his bedroom laughin' as they go through him and Nichole's personal shit.

The detectives searched the house for another 2 hours or so, then here comes McPherson…

"Who's are these," McPherson said, tossin' a package of unused syringes on the kitchen table. "These are probably what your wife uses to knock her victims out before she slits their throats huh?" McPherson said with a crooked ass grin on his face.

"I don't know what the fuck you talkin' 'bout," Dubb responded wonderin' what the fuck Nikki was doin' with a pack of syringes in the house.

"I take it you don't know anything about this either then, do you?" McPherson asked, settin' about a quarter ounce of weed on the kitchen table.

"That shit's mine," Dubb responded, showin' no emotion or fear without blinkin' an eye.

"We don't have to worry about this lil' bag right here, all I need from you is…"

"Hold up homeboy, stop right there. C'mon you can hurry *up* and get me down to the station. You got me fucked up, I ain't got shit else to say," Dubb said, risin' from the table, turnin' around placin' his hands behind his back.

CHAPTER 80

Outside Bryan's crib.....

This is Tricia Ramsey and I'm filling in for Deborah Caldwell. She was injured in the explosion that took place earlier inside the house of Detective Bryan Wilkins. At least 3 dozen agents were killed in the blast and several other agents outside the home were injured from trajectories' ejected by the force of the explosion. We have word that all of the agents were killed but there is not an exact body count and authorities won't release the identity of the victims until their families have been notified. There has been a new development in the case. Homicide detective Craig Garner released a statement saying that the person they believe to be the Snitch Killer has been taken into custody. Law enforcement personnel are currently executing a search on the home of 27 year old Nichole Williams. Mrs. Williams has been charged in the murders and is currently being interviewed by detectives. Her husband, convicted drug dealer Ryan "R-Dubb" Williams was arrested on marijuana charges as a result of the search. This is Tricia Ramsey reporting for WBN News live on Channel 5. We'll give it to you first as the story develops," the perky lil' news reporter said with a smile.

CHAPTER 81

The Lake County Jail....

"You have two minutes," the overweight jail guard said as he led Ryan to the phone.....

"Hello, who dis callin' me from jail?" Alexis asked.

"It's Dubb, how you know I'm callin' from jail?"

"Boy boo, many times as Ayzia done called my phone from that number? I know it by heart. What's wrong, where's Nikki?"

"Shit's fucked up. They arrested her for all them murders," Dubb responded, still unable to believe this shit.

"What? Aw man, oh my God. What the.......aww, hell naw," Alexis said, soundin' like she's 'bout to have a nervous breakdown.

"Listen, listen. My bond is only $800. Come get me so we can work on getting' her up out this bitch," Dubb said.

"I'm on my way. I'm comin' right now," Alexis said, grabbin' her purse and headin' for the door.

CHAPTER 82

Meanwhile……

"……..Nichole, they're going to give you the needle and I don't want to see that happen to you," Detective Patricia Ellis said, still tryin' to sweet talk Nichole into sayin' somethin'. They figured it would be easier to break her if they used a female to go in and engage in a lil' "girl talk".

"You really love him don't you?" Detective Ellis asked.

"Umm, I'm not trying to be rude or anything, but I asked for a lawyer about an hour ago. Why are you still talkin' to me?" Nikki asked politely.

"Look honey," Ellis said, reaching out and touchin' Nikki's hand. "I know the effect a man can have on a woman," the detective continued, ignoring Nichole's requests for legal representation. "I once had a man I'd do anything for. I loved him so much," Ellis said with sentiment like she was really reflecting on an old flame she had.

"What happened?" Nikki asked.

"He ran up my credit and fucked my best friend," the detective said as her and Nichole busted out laughin'

"Look babe, I understand why you did it, especially Norman Sanders. That piece of shit's a low-life scum bag. You couldn't take going through another trial so you killed him. See, we figured it aaalll out….," the detective paused to let her words sink in.

"All of the informants, except for the one you shot, had traces of a very potent tranquilizer in their blood. And that tranquilizer diluted with a saline solution is used by your hospital on your wing to sedate rowdy children who try to refuse treatment, but if it's used in a higher concentrated dosage, it can knock a 230 pound man unconscious in a matter of seconds. You're a woman, you're not strong enough to overpower your victims. You had to disable them first. And Sanders, he was last seen driving from Smitty's with a woman matching your description. I can help you. We know Ryan is very influential and controlling. We know his brother Bryan told him who the informants were. Then Ryan tricked you into killing them. We'll back you, you were mentally ill, temporarily insane. We have the plea bargain ready," Patricia said, lookin' down at her Blackberry, readin' a text.....

"See there, he's not going to wait for you. He doesn't love you. We arrested him for possession of marijuana and *your* best friend just posted his bond. He's gonna run away with her and forget all about you. You know, they found your syringes. He told us they were yours and he gave a statement implicating you in the murders. Why would you protect him? All you have to do is sign this statement on camera saying your husband got his information from Bryan and that you were coerced into killing the informants. You'll do 5, maybe 7 years in a mental institution. You are madly in love and you killed all those informants to protect your husband."

You gotdamn right! And if your ass knew what I'm sittin' here thinkin' about doin' to you for lying, talkin' about my husband gave a statement, you'd get the fuck out my face. The Snitch Killer thought to herself.......

"Excuse me, I appreciate the lil' girly talk and everything, but you are sadly mistaken. I have no idea what you're talkin' about. I'm a law abiding citizen. I'm a nurse. I take care of sick children for a living. And far as my husband Ryan is concerned, married or not, if I knew about any illegal activity, I would turn him in. Thank you for your time Ms. Ellis. Now please, I would like to consult with an attorney. I have nothing else to say," Nichole said very politely. She's seen too many movies. She knows these interview tapes make their way into the courtroom and the jury judges the demeanor of the suspect. She got her game plan tight. She knows they have no statements and no witnesses. She worked alone and she never told anyone. She was always extra careful not to leave any DNA behind and she killed Mean Geraldine. All she gotta do is keep her mouth shut and play the innocent, sweet, caring lil' nurse who takes care of sick children for a living. So what, they found a new pack of syringes, *and*? She's a nurse, and hell, her hospital ain't the only place you can get that tranquilizer....

"You know, once I leave here, the state is going to push for the death penalty. It's now or never."

"I really wish I could help you. I really do. I know you've been workin' hard and I hope you find your killer. This is all a big mistake. Now please, I need to see a lawyer. I would like to go home and fix my husband some lunch," Nikki said as she reached out and touched the detective's hand.

"Well you won't ever be doin' that again. All deals are off. I'll see you in court," Detective Ellis said, getting up from the table and leavin' the room. She even paused at the door a second to see if Nichole would try to stop her and make a deal like most suspects do at this point. But not Nikki, baby girl wouldn't budge.

CHAPTER 83

Home alone.....

"Man, this is some muh fuckin' bullshit," Dubb said as he was finishin' up in the bedroom. Seems like they just trashed the place, focusin' more on tearin' up the crib than on really findin' somethin'. "Fuck!" he yelled to himself, cause ain't nobody in the house but him. Nichole ain't been gone a whole day and already the house feels so empty, and so lonely. Nichole is his everything and he feels like if she ain't out here wit' him, he might as well be locked up his damn self. That's his baby, his boo boo, his hunni bunni. She's the reason why he wants to turn his life around and get out the game. And them bitches crazy if they think for a *second* he's gonna sit still and let them take her from him, and just when the nigga thought he wasn't gonna be able to breathe anymore.....She called.

"Hello?" Ryan said out of breath as his heart tried to beat out of his chest.

"Hey," Nikki responded, feeln' the exact same way, experiencin' relief at just the sound of her husband's voice.

"Are you okay in there? Didn't none of them put they hands on you did they?"

"No, I'm okay," she responded.

"Now look baby, first thing tomorrow, I'm going to go get you a lawyer. I'm getting' Joseph Dershowitz, he's the best lawyer in the area. Murder cases are what he specializes in. He be practicin' in Chicago too. He ain't never lost a murder case. Did they try to talk to you?" Dubb asked.

"Yeah, they sent some lady detective in to talk to me. She stayed in that room talkin' to me for like a couple hours...."

"What did you say?" Dubb asked, cuttin' her off.

"Nothin', it ain't nothin' to tell her. I ain't did nothin'," Nichole said, knowin' the call is being recorded.

"Cool, now when they move you into the block, don't talk to none of them bitches about your case—none of 'em! One of them ho's be done popped up on the witness stand tryin' to win a "get out of jail free" card. Go to the bitch that's runnin' a store and get everything you need, I'll run right down there and put the money on her books and fatten your shit up at the same time. Don't worry about shit. I got you."

"Okay, umm, who bonded you out?"

"Alexis," Dubb responded.

"Nigga, what the fuck I tell you!" Nichole snapped, jealous that Alexis was even able to share the same air as her husband while she can't even be blessed with his presence. "Didn't I tell you not to never call her again?"

"Who else was I gonna call to come pick me up? You trippin'."

"Well, I done told you. Play wit' me if you want to..."

"Look girl," Dubb cut her off. "We ain't got time for all this trippin' and shit. All I'm worried about is gettin' you home. Just try to relax. I'm going to make sure you get up outta there."

"I'm sorry, I just don't want you out there fuckin' other bitches while I'm in here lookin' stupid."

"Look baby, I would never play you like that. You the love of my life. Can't nobody ever take your place. I'm finna hold you down the same way you held me down," Dubb responded to her.

"You promise?" Nikki asked.

"Your time's up Mrs. Williams," the jail guard said.

"I gotta go, do you promise?" Nikki asked more aggressively.

"Baby, I swear," Dubb responded. "I love you."

"I love you too," Nichole said as they hung up wit' tears in their eyes. Each one of them not even knowin' the other one is cryin'.

CHAPTER 84

Monday Morning……

First thing, Ryan damn near did a karate flip up out the bed and went to the health club to get some money and the key Bryan gave him. Then he headed strait to Joseph Dershowitz's law office on the north side of Chicago. Dershowitz's one of those greedy ass Jewish lawyers. And by no means is this said in an offensive manner. It's said as a compliment. Them Jewish lawyers is about they money. You put that money in they hand and they go handle that bid'ness…..

"Excuse me ma'am. I'm here to see Mr. Dershowitz," Dubb said as he approached the receptionist desk of the swanky law firm. *It looks like it costs money just to walk up in this bitch.* Dubb thought as he gripped the strap of the leather duffle bag held to his side.

"Do you have an appointment?" the beautiful receptionist asked, showin' off a set of perfect teeth.

"No, ma'am, I don't," Dubb responded.

"Okay, well let's get you one," the receptionist said, flippin' through a large appointment book. "It looks like ummm, we can squeeze you in after the first of the year," she said as she moved her pen down the appointment book.

"Uh ma'am, I'm sorry but I need to see him now—today," Dubb said impatiently as he looked around the corner of receptionist station at the door with Mr. Dershowitz's name on it.

"Well, I'm sorry sir, that won't be possible. If you'd like, I'll take your name and number and I'll have Mr. Dershowitz give you a call later this afternoon."

"That's okay," Dubb said as the gangsta in him pulled him around the corner and right into Mr. Dershowitz office....

"What the hell are you doin' in my office?" Dershowitz asked as he stood, pickin' up the phone.

"I-I couldn't stop him," the receptionist said, runnin' in behind Dubb.

"Now hold on, I'm here to hire you," Dubb said, dumpin' stacks of 50's and 100's on Dershowitz's desk.

"Well why didn't you say so. Have a seat, uh, Mr., umm, what's your name?" Mr. Dershowitz asked, motioning to the large leather chair across from his desk.

"Mr. Williams," Dubb answered as him and Mr. Dershowitz shook hands.

"We're fine Sandra," Mr. Dershowitz said, dismissin' her.

"Now, what can I do for Mr. Williams today?" Dershowitz asked, glancin' at the pile of money sittin' on his desk as the receptionist closed the door.

"I need you to get my wife out of jail."

"Okay? What's she charged with? You'd think she killed somebody the way you barged in here throwin' money on my desk," Dershowitz said, grabbin' a yellow legal pad preparin' to take notes.

"She's charged with the snitch killings."

"Holy Moses!" Dershowitz responded, droppin' his pen. "Well, I charge a hundred thousand dollars. I need seventy-five up front..."

"You got a hundred and fifty thousand in front of you. It's yours. Make her your priority. They don't have anything on her. They just fishin'."

"This is going to be an interesting case. I'll tell you what, give me her full name and I'll go see her today and I'll drop by the prosecutor's office. Come back tomorrow at 2 o'clock, and I'll let you know what's goin' on."

"Her name is Nichole Lynette Williams, and she's in the Lake County Jail."

"It's none of my business where all this cash comes from. If the wrong people knew you just dropped 150K on my desk, you'd have some explaining to do," Dershowitz said as he buzzed his receptionist.

"Sandy, write Mr. Williams a receipt that says paid in full, trial rate for a murder case......no.......no dollar amount on the receipt," Dershowitz said, hangin' up the receiver. "Stop by the receptionist desk and I'll see you tomorrow at 2," Dershowitz said, shakin' Dubb's hand again as he rose to leave.

Dubb left the lawyer's office with his wife on his mind as he headed to U-store in Merrillville....

CHAPTER 85

Lake County Jail.....

"Chaow time laydee's!" the guard yelled into the block, openin' the food slot to serve lunch to the ladies. Nichole fell in line with the other chicks to get her tray. After receivin' the slop they had the mitigated gall to attempt to call nacho casserole, Nikki returned to her cell sittin' on her bunk Indian style pickin' over the fruit. The shit look and smelled like some canned dog food smeared over some stale tortilla chips wit' a lil' shredded cheese and a few jalapeno peppers on top. Nikki has been pretty quiet. She's hardly spoken two words to anybody since she been in the block. She's stressed out and heartbroken wonderin' if Dubb's with some other bitch, askin' herself if it was all worth it. She'd do just about anything to see Dubb succeed and she's proven it. She's killed 9 people for this nigga. That detective was right, she couldn't go through another trial. The first trial was so lopsided and crooked she damn near had a nervous breakdown in the courtroom and his lawyer ain't really even try to fight his case. He just went along wit' the shit. So, after Ryan got his conviction overturned, she hunted Norman Sanders down.....

"Hey Big Daddy, where you goin'?" Nichole asked, struttin' up to Norman's car dressed like a hooker in loud makeup and a kinky blonde wig as he left Smitty's Sports Bar up on Broadway.

"Back to the house sweet thang, you workin'?" Norman responded thinkin', damn, she looks familiar.

"You payin'?" she smiled, poppin' her gum, twirlin' her wig.

"Get in," the snitchin' ass nigga said. Nichole got in the ride and they drove back to Norman's sister's house where his broke ass was stayin' at the time. Norman opened the door and let her into the small cottage style, 2 bedroom house, and once they got to Norman's bedroom.....

"Get naked Daddy, I'm 'bout to put you to sleep," Nichole said sexily as she placed her purse on the dresser and kicked off her heels.

"Hell yeah bitch, I'm gonna make YOU wanna pay ME," Norman said, undressing as Nichole reached down in her purse and at the right moment, when the nigga was off balance, stumblin' tryin' to get his feet out of his pants while they were bunched around his ankles.......

"Hey bitch! You eatin' my tray," Big Rhonda said, steppin' into the cell, snappin' Nikki out of her daze. Rhonda the block bully. Big, fat, tall, ugly, black ass bitch. Ho looks like the late Notorious BIG in the face.

"This tray?" Nicole said, pointin' to the tray in her lap. "I'm sorry, here let me give it to you," Nichole said politely as she rose off the bed throwin' food in Rhonda's face, cockin' the hard thick plastic tray all the way back like a softball bat, takin' a full swing and smashin' Rhonda's nose as blood splattered on the wall.

"Aaaaagh," Rhonda screamed as her big, fat, black nasty ass fell on the floor.

"Here you go bitch," Nichole said as she stomped that cow in the head. "You-got-me-fucked-up!" Nichole said as she continued to stomp her. Somehow, Rhonda was able to make it to her knees and tried to crawl out of Nikki's cell.

"Unn unh bitch, you forgot your tray," Nikki said, grabbin' her by the legs of her jumpsuit, pullin' her back into the cell and repeatedly kickin' and screamin' at her as she threw food in the bitch's face. Nikki was up in the cell spazzin' out until two bitches ran up in there and pulled her off.

"Get the fuck off me!" Nikki screamed as she flung them ho's off her," I don't know ya'll bitches, get the fuck off me!"

"Chill homegirl. We don't want no smoke. You finna kill that bitch," one of the girls said. "Now calm down," she said as Big Rhonda scooted out the cell and was helped to her feet by a few of the other girls who looked at Nikki in shock. Nikki would've stomped that ho to death if her cellmate Samantha and this white chick named Megan wouldn't have stopped her....

"Fuck that bitch, talkin' 'bout I'm eatin' her tray, nasty ass shit. If she would've asked, I'd gave her the shit," Nichole said as her and Samantha cleaned up the mess she made in their cell.

"Girl, you wild," Samantha said shakin' her head. Samantha's a dark skinned chick from the valley. She's locked up for slashin' a bitch face over her nigga. "What's yo' name chile?"

"Nichole Williams, I'm married to R-Dubb."

"Shud-up! You, you married to R-Dubb? That's my nigga! All is well sista," Samantha said givin' Nikki a hug.

"Almighty," Nikki said, unsure how to respond, rememberin' hearin' Dubb respond like that.

"Hold on," Samantha said, lettin' Nikki go. "You just hold the fuck up, one-minute sista. *You* the one been killin' all them snitches," Samantha whispered in shock, happy to be in the presence of the Snitch Killer. You would've thought she just met Keyshia Cole or some muh fuckin' body.

"I ain't killed nobody, these bitches got me confused wit' somebody else."

"Look baby girl, I feel you. Don't admit to shit. Some of these ho's be done wrote a statement on you. Watch what you say. Never claim that shit, you hear me? To me or nobody else, matter-of-fact, we won't talk about it no mo'," Samantha said wipin' up the last of the food and blood on the floor.

"But, I didn't do nothin'," Nichole said, lookin' like an innocent lil' angel again.

"Good girl," Samantha responded……

CHAPTER 86

The key.....

Dubb was gettin' frustrated as he drove Nikki's Aurora through the rows of storage sheds tryin' to find 4606 F. After being lost in the maze of little buildings and garages, he finally found it.....

What the fuck this nigga give me this key for? Dubb thought to himself as he raised the door of the storage shed to see couches, chairs and other miscellaneous furniture. After movin' shit around a lil' bit and pullin' an old dusty tarp back, there it was. A row of duffel bags filled wit' bundles of hydro, bags of x-pills, kilo's of cocaine, and stacks of money. *SHIT!* He thought to himself as he cut on some lights his brother had plugged into a battery powered generator. After a lil diggin', Dubb discovered that Bryan had left him a note inside one of the duffel bags filled wit' money......

If you readin' this letter shit's fucked up. I'm gone and I ain't never comin' back. All the dope is yours. There's 5 million in these bags. Take 2 ½ million to Aunt Evelynn. She knows who to take it to, they gonna get Uncle Nook out, and he'll have a million to chill wit'. Take all the rest of this shit and get the fuck outta town. Move somewhere quiet with Nikki and have some bad ass lil' kids.

Love ya bruh,

Bryan

DAMN Dubb thought to himself, wonderin' what the fuck Bryan means, "I ain't comin' back." Not wastin' any time, he figured out the money was packaged in blocks of a hundred G's. He took the duffel bags stuffed with 2 ½ million dollars and threw 'em in the car, cut out the lights, locked the shed up and headed strait to Aunt Evelynn's house....

CHAPTER 87

The Lake County Courthouse.....

"Alright Phil, tell me what you got on the snitch killer case. I'm representin' her. I just filed my appearance," Dershowitz asked as he bumped into Philip Hawthorn, the deputy prosecutor handlin' the case on his way out of the courthouse.

"We have an eyewitness who says he seen Norman Sanders leave the sports bar with your client."

"Was this witness intoxicated. I mean, he was at the bar right?"

"You're going to have to wait on discovery," Hawthorn responded.

"Okay then, what else you got?"

"Well, all the victims except for one was found with a powerful tranquilizer in their blood stream, and this tranquilizer is easily accessible to your client. She works as a nurse at a Methodist Hospital in Merrillville. She's a woman. We believe since she couldn't overpower her victims, she knocked 'em out wit' the tranquilizer, then she slit their throats.

"Any prints?" Dershowitz asked.

"No."

"Find any syringes at the scene."

"No, but we found a whole pack of 'em in her bedroom," Hawthorn responded.

"She's a nurse."

"My point exactly," the prosecutor responded.

"So wait a second, you mean to tell me you're holding my client on multiple counts of murder based upon one probably intoxicated eyewitness that Norman Sanders was seen leaving a bar with my client. All the victims except for one had traces of a tranquilizer in their bloodstream. My client has access to it and you found some unused syringes, and oh, this *theory* that the killer's a woman since the victims were drugged?"

"Don't forget, all the informants were informing on her husband, that's motive," the prosecutor responded with confidence.

"It still doesn't mean *she's* the killer. You're building a case solely upon circumstantial evidence."

"I've won murder trials on circumstantial evidence before," Hawthorn shot at him.

"Not with me on the case you haven't," Dershowitz shot right back.

"Look, she wouldn't speak to the detectives. Why don't we set up a meeting and have her explain her whereabouts during the time of the murders."

"I don't think so Phillip."

"I'll tell you what. Have her submit to a polygraph test. If she passes, we'll let her go," Hawthorn said.

"And use everything she says against her if she doesn't. Absolutely not. I'll tell *you* what. Save yourself the lawsuit and the embarrassment, release my client. I'm filin' a Motion to Dismiss this afternoon. C'mon Phillip, you guys have nothing on her. Ya'll rushed to make an arrest because too much pressure was on you. Produce some evidence or let her go," Dershowitz said.

"The gloves are comin' off. This is a highly political case. It's getting national attention. An informant dead on the courthouse lawn? Somebody has to pay for that shit. So file your motion. The court is not going for your pre-trial antics on this one. You're right, it's too much pressure."

"See you at trial," Dershowtiz said as he walked away, headed to the Lake County Jail to see his new client.

CHAPTER 88

Later That Afternoon.....

"Hello?" Dubb answered the phone as he was sittin' on the couch watchin' T.V.

"You have a call from the Lake County Jail. This is a pre-paid call. To accept, press 1, to decline, press 5," the automated voice said.

"Hey," Nicole said, soundin' a lil' down.

"Baby, what's wrong?"

"The lawyer just left."

"What he say?" Ryan asked, not wantin' to wait any longer to hear the news.

"He told me not to talk on this phone. He said ya'll have an appointment tomorrow and he'll tell you then. But I will say that I'm goin' to trial and I might have to sit in here for a year or two waitin' on the court date. Can you wait that long, you gonna ride this shit out wit' me?" Nichole asked, mockin' him. That's the same shit he was askin' her when he got caught up.

"I don't care *how* long it takes, I don't care if them white folks give you a hundred years. I'll be right here," Dubb shot the same shit she said to him the day he got found guilty.

"Boy you crazy," Nichole laughed at him.

"What's up wit' ya, I put $500 on your books today, did

you borrow all the shit you need?"

"Yeah, you got a pen?" Nikki asked.

"Yep, hold on," Dubb said, reachin' for one on the end table. "Okay, go ahead," he said, ready to write.

"Megan Satterfield, I need you to send her $70. She didn't even charge me shit. She just wants me to pay her back. I got some food, some soap and toothpaste-n-shit and some phone cards."

"That's cool, she sounds like a white chick."

"Yeah, she's a Paris Hilton type chick. She keeps getting' locked up for drunk drivin' and cocaine possession. Her daddy 'nem got money. They kept buyin' her way out of trouble. The judge got tired of seein' her ass and violated her probation," Nikki explained.

"What else been goin' on?

"Well, this big bitch tried to punk me out my tray. I got her mind right for her though, yeah she cool now," Nichole said.

"Hell naw, you crazy," Dubb said, crackin' up.

"Aw yeah, you know a bitch named Samantha Jones from the Valley?"

"Yeah, why?"

"Did you used to fuck her? She said she knows you. How you know her? Don't have no bitches all in my face you used to fuck actin' all fake-n-shit."

"Girl, you trippin' I know her brothers-n-shit. Her whole family's Vice Lords. She's good people," Ryan explained.

"You have 1 minute remaining," the automated voice said.

"Well shit, the phone's finna hang up, call me back." Dubb said.

"I'm used to acceptin' *your* calls, not you acceptin' *mine*, this crazy. I love you though," Nichole said, soundin' depressed again.

"Everything's gonna be okay, I love you too," he responded as they disconnected. Nichole called right back. And just like when Dubb was locked up, they sat and talked on the phone all day like two teenagers in love who were forbidden to see each other......

CHAPTER 89

Tuesday 2:00 p.m., Mr. Dershowitz's Office.....

"C'mon in, have a seat," Dershowitz said, shakin' Dubb's hand as he sat down.

"So what's goin' on?" Dubb asked, anxious to know his wife's fate.

"They don't have a case, it's all circumstantial but they're going to *try* to make an example out of your wife. We have a fight on our hands."

"Do you think, I mean, can you beat it, Dubb asked, feelin' discouraged.

"Young man, I've *never* lost a murder trial and I don't intend to start. I need to see the state's discovery. As you already know, it will tell us exactly what they have and I'll build our defense from there. With no physical evidence and no eye witnesses, they're going to have a very difficult time. We just might have a long road ahead of us."

"So what are you going to do?" Dubb asked.

"It's what I *did* my friend. Yesterday, I filed for discovery. I filed a Motion to Dismiss and for a Fast and Speedy Trial. We're going to pressure *them*. We're not going to sit back and let them build their case for a year or two. If the Motion to Dismiss doesn't go well, they'll have to hurry up and scramble for a trial they can't possibly get ready for."

"If you filed for a fast and speedy trial, why could it take up to a year," Dubb asked.

"They got ways to wiggle around it. My whole strategy for filing fast and speedy is to make them produce their evidence *now*. We'll see everything they got this Monday at the hearing. This case is political. With the informant being found at the courthouse, *somebody* had to get arrested, quick."

"Ok, well thanks a lot Mr. Dershowitz," Dubb rose to shake his hand, unsure of how things are going to turn out.

"Oh yeah, I almost forgot, I went to see her yesterday. You have a beautiful wife. She seems like a nice person. She gave me this note to give to you. She said it was important and she couldn't send it in the mail or say it over the phone. I never gave this to you," Dershowitz said, handin' Dubb the envelope.

"Thanks Mr. Dershowitz," Dubb said as he rose to leave the office.

"Don't forget about the hearing this Monday at 9:00 a.m.," Dershowitz said as Dubb left the office.

Dubb sat in Nikki's Aurora, feelin' like all this shit is his fault, wonderin' if Nichole's ever gonna get to come home. That nigga'll spend every cent of the 4.1 million dollars they have tryin' to bring her home. He was so upset he almost forgot about the note she sent to him.....

I kept all those snitches off your ass so you could be free. I'm in here for you nigga. Handle your business and hold me down 'til I get home. I swear to God, if you cheat on me, I will kill you. Bitch, I ain't playin'! Hopefully by now you see I'm serious. Stay away from Alexis and be good. I love you and I miss you so much. P.S. Don't forget to take out the trash.

This bitch crazy Dubb said, shakin' his head as he tore the note in tiny pieces, pullin' out the parkin' lot, holdin' his hand out the window lettin' all the bits of paper blow in the wind.

CHAPTER 90

Tuesday Night.....

".......you're so sweet," the full figured middle aged white woman giggled as she sipped wine and ate cheese with her man by the fireplace. She's kinda chubby, but pretty as hell with platinum blonde hair and big 'ole titties.

"Unn unnnnh, you're the one that's sweet momma!" he responded nibbling on her neck, takin' in the sweet fragrance of her bath and body works scented lotion as they were warmed by the heat of the flames.

"I just love it out here in the wild. The nature just does somethin' to me. I loves me a mountain man," she said, runnin' her pretty lil' fingers through his beard.

"Do ya darlin'? You love you a wild, untamed *mountain* man? C'mere girl, AAARGH!" he growled like an animal playfully biting at her leg as she screamed and giggled tryin' to scoot away from him. "I'll tell you what," he said as he laid on top of her, propped up on his arms and plantin' lil' kisses on her cheeks, her lips, and her neck.

"What's that tiger," she asked.

"Why don't you go slip into somethin' a bit more comfortable while I go out and fetch us some more wood for the fire, then I'm gonna come back in here and skin you right here, on this here bear rug," he said as he tickled her and kissed her deeply.

"Okay, hurry back, I might get lonely," she said with a

sexy lil 'smile.

"I'll be right back momma," he said, getting' up puttin' his boots on, headed for the back door of the cabin. He heard coyotes howlin' at the moon on this chilly winter night. *It's a beautiful clear sky*. He thought to himself as he looked up at the stars....

"You're a mutha fuckin' rat. Cops don't squeal on other cops," Bryan said, stickin' his Glock .45 semi automatic pistol in the back of Charlie's neck. "I thought we took care of our own," Bryan said, poking the pistol deeper.

"It's alright," Charlie said with his hands up. "I knew this was comin', I knew this was gonna happen when I fucked you over. I'm sorry man, I really am. Do what you came to do. I'm ready to meet my maker," Charlie said as he held his head to the sky callin' on Jesus, Mary, Joseph, the Holy Spirit, and everybody else he thought could help him.

"Click-Clack!" came the sound of a shot gun from the back door.

"Drop your fucking pistol," Agent Pauline Whitfield said with a heavy Kentucky accent as she stood in the doorway in a black negligee' and high heels. Big sexy bitch! The Feds use her to investigate backwoods marijuana farmers and hillbillies who run illegal moonshine operations that span throughout the mountain states. Any time a country ass white woman is needed they call Pauline.

"I'll knock that big noggin' of yours plum off your shoulders. Now fuckin' drop it," she said, lookin' down the barrel of the shotgun wit' Bryan's head dead in her sights.

"Pop!" the 45 barked as the front of Charlie's face exploded from Bryan shootin' him in the back of the head. Fuck that shit, he came here on a suicide mission. He never planned to get away. Prison ain't no place for a cop no matter *how* dirty he is. As he turned his gun to fire at Agent Whitfield....

"Ka-boooooom!" the big Dolly Parton lookin' ass bitch hit him with a deer slug dead in the face.

CHAPTER 91

A Week Later.....

This morning, suspected serial killer Nichole Lynettte Williams was cleared in the Snitch Killings. After arguments made by her high profile defense attorney, Joseph Dershowitz, she was ordered to be released from the Lake County Jail just moments ago. Prosecutors state that there just wasn't any evidence linking her to the crimes. However, they believe justice has been served. They believe the real killer, Bryan Wilkins, was killed by Federal Agent Pauline Whitfield during a standoff. Bryan Wilkins was holding a gun to the head of Charles McGregor. Mr. McGregor was the evidence room attendant for the joint Metropolitan Task Force. During a federal investigation into allegations that members of the task force were taking narcotics out of evidence and distributing them among local dealers, McGregor became an informant to avoid federal prosecution. Ultimately, Sergeant Wilkins shot McGregor in the head, thus forcing Agent Whitfield to fire her weapon in return. Mr. Wilkins was also suspected in the mysterious disappearance of federal agent Amber Locke. Also, top story at 5, Nichole Williams isn't the only member of the Williams family being released from custody. Judge Oliver Herschburger has agreed to modify the sentence of Ned "Nookie" Williams. Williams was convicted in 1978 for killing off-duty Chicago police officer Albert Johnson in broad daylight outside a Gary pool hall. He was sentenced to life without parole. Williams' attorney argued that under new sentencing guidelines, Williams should receive the maximum sentence of 65 years. His attorney stated also that he does not qualify for life without parole because Johnson was not in uniform and Williams did not knowingly kill an officer of the law. Williams was resentenced to the maximum of 65 years. Due to college courses Williams recently completed in prison, he is set to receive a time-cut that will set him free in the next couple weeks. We'll have more for you at 5. This is Tricia Ramsey reporting live for WBN Channel 5."

EPILOGUE

A month later outside the Body Tap Strip Club in Atlanta, Georgia....

As Alexis opened the car door and sat her lil' sexy ass on the plush leather seats, she heard her homegirl's annoying voice....

"Bitch, you got my money?"

Made in the USA
Charleston, SC
02 February 2012